Nashville
By Morning

MAXINE DOUGLAS

Nashville by Morning

by Maxine Douglas

Copyright 2007, 2013 © Debbie Fritter

All Rights Reserved

Cover Design by Ramona

Edited by LE Leonard

Published by D.H. Fritter

ISBN-10: 1500737631
ISBN-13: 978-1500737634

DEDICATION

The last week of September 2008 we lost a young family member. Tiffany was only 18 years old when she took her place beside God. She is missed by her family and friends, and all those she touched. This book is dedicated in her memory.

In Memory of

Tiffany Marie Dutcher

March 15, 1990 – September 19, 2008

Gone by never forgotten as you live in all our hearts!

CONTENTS

ACKNOWLEDGMENTS

"If you would not be forgotten as soon as you are dead,
either write something worth reading or do things worth
writing."
~~ Benjamin Franklin ~~

An author is sometimes alone in his or her world trying to sort things out. Once in a while she will re-enter the here and now, to call upon her fellow authors, friends, and family, hoping that maybe, just maybe, they'll have a notion where she's been or where she's going.

My friend and Romance Author, Callie Hutton, without her encouragement and handholding, I never would have ventured out on this journey. Thank you Callie for never being too busy to answer my hundreds, make that thousands, of questions.

My best-friend in life, my husband, never wavers in his support as I pursue a writing career. He's always here to give me an honest opinion—whether I agreed with it or not.

To my readers, like you, who travel with me into my many worlds and hopefully give you a few moments in someone else's shoes.

ChapterOne

Heather Jones hadn't really paid that much attention to the inside of Gabe's before. Now, she soaked in the autographed pictures that hung on almost every wall. Traditional artists like Jeanne Seeley, George Riddle, and Bill Carlisle were among the parade of stars that frequented the club, and with the hotel right behind a line of trees in the back, many of the tourists came wandering in after the Opry. It could get pretty crowded, and tonight was no exception.

Her cousins, Rona and Robert, finally danced their way off the floor around midnight, making their way over to her. "I think we're going home. It's near midnight and we both have to work tomorrow. You can come along or stay, it's totally up to you." Rona leaned closer. "Frank has agreed to give you a lift, if you need one." Her warm, mischievous tone left no doubt as to her hopes for Heather and Frank, the owner of the bar.

"Ah, yeah. I get the message. Just make sure you're all done making love noises by the time I get there." Heather winked, knowing Rona appreciated her staying longer. "Why don't I go home with you and bring the car back; it's only a few blocks. I don't want to rely on someone I barely know to give me a ride."

"Frank can be trusted; otherwise we wouldn't leave you in his care." Rona grabbed Robert by the arm, tugging him off his stool. "Just have fun. The door will be open for you."

Heather waved her off with a flick of the wrist. "Just get outta here."

Rona's right. If I'm going to start a new life, I have to take the training wheels off sometime. Might as well be tonight.

After all, she couldn't depend on them being her body guards for the rest of her life.

She was about to look for Frank when the opening chords of "Feels so Right" came on and she felt a presence next to her.

Frank held his hand out to her. "Come on, Yank. You need to get off that stool for a while."

She placed her hand in Frank's and allowed him to lead her on to the dance floor. Frank slipped an arm around her waist, taking her other hand, and pulled her close enough for her to feel his heart beating. She fit against his six-foot frame with ease. Even his ever-present cowboy hat didn't budge from its perch.

Fighting nervousness, Heather took a deep breath. "Rona said you were going to give me a ride home tonight. I hope it's not too much of a hassle for you." She watched his hazel eyes for any sign of a lie as he replied. She was relieved to know she'd not be a burden on someone she'd just met.

He loosened his hold on her waist a bit, giving her room to actually breathe. "It's a good opportunity for us to get to know each other. Your cousins never really give out much information; they're pretty tight-lipped about family." He swung her around and then pulled her close to him again. The neatly trimmed mustache curved around his mouth, the color matching his collar-length chestnut-brown hair.

"Besides, they needed some time to do what couples do. They thought it would give you a chance to spread your wings a bit." He smiled, his hazel eyes sparkling.

Heather felt slightly irritated her cousin assumed she'd go along with her little plan. "Spread my wings? Do they think I'm a little social butterfly in search of a place to land?"

Spinning her around to the last chord of the song, he laughed, warming her heart. "Nope, they just want you to have fun." He led her back to her stool at the bar and then returned to the stage and his place behind the drums.

Despite Frank's friendliness, something inside told Heather he couldn't be anything more than a friend. She had more pressing issues to deal with like finding a job and working on her songwriting. *Forget a relationship.*

She'd rather write about pain and heartache than experience it.

****

When Frank finally got the last of the customers out the door, it was three o'clock in the morning. He wanted to get to bed sometime before the sun came up. Why he'd agreed to look after Heather was beyond him. He didn't really like being a babysitter for a newcomer on a work night.

Opening up a bottle of wine, he half filled two glasses. "Welcome to Nashville, Heather. I hope all your dreams come true."

She raised her glass. "Thanks, Frank. I really do hope everything works out. Only time will tell, as you well know."

He watched her sip the wine, a wistful look floating in her eyes. *Hell!* "What is it you're looking for? The music business is hard on a person. Sometimes it wrecks their life."

She took another sip, a smile at the corners of her mouth. "What

4

everyone wants…their dreams to come true. I know I don't want the same-old-same-old; you know—the boring housewife routine. I want to be a success and make my family proud that I took a chance. That I…"

Frank felt himself drawn closer to Heather. He'd been around enough to know she was here trying to accomplish what most musicians in Nashville dreamed of. Maybe in time, she'd reveal more of what she wanted. He had a feeling there was more to it than what she was willing to tell at this point.

"You must think I'm a pea brain for wanting something so bad I'd change my whole way of life to achieve it." She finished off her wine, resting her head on one hand. "I guess I want it all." Tears brimmed in her eyes.

Frank knew the hurt she was feeling from wanting something so bad you'd leave your family for it. *Maybe I can help her a little, point her in the right direction. Shadow Records is looking for new prospects again.*

Somehow this Yankee woman already warmed a place in his heart. She reminded him of the dreams and hopes that had driven him to Nashville in the first place. In her simple manner, she'd awakened a sleeping lion he'd long forgotten lived in him.

Chapter Two

It had to be at least eighty degrees on this April morning. On Heather's way back from what seemed like the hundredth disastrous interview, she felt like a deflated balloon. The story was always the same. She had the skills and experience necessary to perform the job, but what she lacked was at least one local job reference.

As she parked Rona's baby-blue Thunderbird in the Ramada Inn parking lot, Heather knew her cousin would be just as disappointed. Finding a suitable job had proven more difficult than either of them had anticipated.

Making her way across the lot and into the hotel's restaurant, Heather glanced at her watch. The lunch crowd wouldn't start coming in for another forty-five minutes. She'd have plenty of time to give Rona another failed report.

"Well, I can tell by the look on your face that you got the same ol' answers again." Rona placed a glass of iced coffee in front of Heather and took the seat opposite her. "But all is *not* lost."

"How can you say that? I've been here for nearly three weeks, and still no job in sight." All her hopes and dreams were about to fly out the door when Betty, the restaurant manager, pulled up a chair.

"Rona's right, you know. Just when everything seems darkest, suddenly a ray of light can be seen." A wry smile lite up her face as if she'd just been told the deepest of secrets.

"Yeah, right." Heather's shoulders slumped. She'd never felt so defeated in her entire life.

Betty pushed an application and pen in front of her. "One of the part-time night hostesses gave notice last night and I need someone who can be trained and start work right away. The job's yours, if you're interested. All you have to do is fill out that application and you could start Monday night."

"If I'm interested? Of course I'm interested. What time on Monday?" Gratitude swam through Heather, replaced by apprehension. "To be honest, I've never done this kind of work before."

"How about four o'clock? That'll give you time to meet the rest of the staff and see where the major things are before the crowd comes in." Betty smiled widely, totally ignoring Heather's confession.

"Great! See you then." Heather sealed the deal by shaking Betty's hand. She knew Rona had been worried about her these past few weeks. Hell, she'd felt the depression starting to set in even before she'd seen the worry in Rona's eyes.

The wind was changing. New horizons were off in the not too distant landscape.

New beginnings.

Chapter Three

A few weeks later…

"What does one wear to the Grand Old Opry?" Rummaging through her dresses, Heather pulled out a short-sleeved tan number. It was simple and hugged her soft curves. "Now, if I can just find those slip-ons…"

Heather was nervous as a cat—almost as nervous as Frank had looked when he'd asked her to go with him tonight. She giggled, thinking how he'd looked like a teenage boy asking a girl out on his first date ever. That seemed ages ago instead of only last week.

The doorbell chimed as she slipped into the pair of brown flats.

"Hi, Robert. Heather ready yet?" Frank's slow southern drawl filtered into her room.

If nothing else, he's punctual. Good-looking helps, too. She laughed inwardly, taking one last look at herself in the mirror.

"Yeah, she ought to be. You know how women are. It takes them hours to get everything just right. Come on in.

"Heather, Frank's here," he hollered.

"Be right there," she called out, wondering whether she should make Frank wait. *Why wait? Friends, nothing more, nothing less.*

Frank was about to sit down when she walked into the living room. This would be the first time he'd see her in something other than jeans. Judging by the expression on his face, she'd have to say he liked what he saw.

"Wow, do you look great." The pleasure shone from Frank's eyes as he took in a side of Heather very few people witnessed. "We've got to leave if we want a good place to park and avoid the line."

Heather smiled, and then turned to Rona. "I'll be back early and give you a full report."

Heather followed Frank out the door. Walking toward his dark blue SUV, she got a strange feeling that tonight wasn't going to be just any night.

****

Opryland was a huge resort located off Briley Parkway. The Opryland Hotel, as well as the Grand Ole Opry House, was essentially part of Nashville's entertainment center. The guest parking lot looked huge and was filling up fast.

Frank drove around to the security post and waited for his name to be found for clearance into the restricted area. Once inside, they were escorted down a couple of corridors, past dressing rooms occupied by their assigned performers, and finally to the left side of the stage.

Stagehands bustled around them, adjusting the sound equipment and lighting. Microphones were checked every few seconds. The excitement of pre-show preparations caught and drew her in.

"This is it, Heather. What just about every country music musician dreams about—performing at the Opry." Frank smiled, his eyes lit up like a Christmas tree. "Fantastic, isn't it?"

"Is it always like this, even if it's not the only show of the day?" she asked, unable to keep her eyes off the goings-on around her. Butterflies fluttered in her stomach as if she was the one getting ready to perform.

"Yup. Doesn't matter if it's the first, second, or even a third performance. Everything still has to be checked and rechecked." Frank took a deep breath, the look on his face wishful.

Celebrities, old and new, milled about. People like Randy Travis, and a group of four guys who reminded her of The Oak Ridge Boys, only William Golden had a long, white beard. And then there was Jeannie Seely, Rascal Flats… The names blurred along with the faces too quickly for Heather to sort them all out in her mind.

Then, unexpectedly, Emerald Braun appeared from the shadows, her legendary guitar slung over a shoulder. Heather had followed her career since Emerald had won Rising Star a few years earlier. The songwriter's love affair with Utah Sheridan graced the tabloids monthly.

"Em!" Frank called out, pulling Heather along with him. "Utah didn't say anything about the two of you being back in town." He dropped Heather's hand to wrap his arms around the songwriter.

Emerald laughed and hugged Frank back. She smiled at Heather and then extended a hand. "Hi. Frank tends to forget to introduce people. I'm Emerald. And you are…?"

Heather shook her hand and sucked in a breath to calm her nerves. "Heather Jones."

"Well, Heather, welcome to Nashville." Emerald turned her attention back to Frank, hugged him one last time, and then hurried back into the shadows.

Heather watched in wonderment as the young woman disappeared from sight. She'd never imagined she'd ever meet someone from her home state there.

"You never told me you knew Emerald Braun." She looked up at Frank and burst out laughing at the glint of humor in his hazel eyes.

"Yeah, well it didn't seem important. Don't worry; you'll be seeing more of her now that they're back in town." Frank took her elbow and led her to a place where they could not only see the performers, but could feel the heat from the lights. She'd be able to see the audience's reaction to every moment once the curtain went up. She'd feel the experience she'd only dreamed about…being on stage at the Grand Ole Opry.

Chapter Four

James Sheridan had been born into the Nashville music scene. His father, Will Sheridan, was well known for his bluegrass music. Like his younger brother Utah, James had lived in that shadow for as long as he could remember. It was proving difficult making the break from bluegrass to country, but all he needed was the right song and, most importantly, right timing.

His younger brother Utah had already broken through after appearing on Nashville Rising Star. James was still waiting for his turn.

I hope tonight will be it.

James's band, The Night Ramblers, was getting ready for an appearance in the Opry. This wasn't their first time on the Opry stage, but tonight was going to be special. James and the boys were going to introduce a new song that could be just the one to break him free of his father's image.

It hadn't been easy growing up as Will Sheridan's son. All his life, James was in the public eye. Not knowing if people kept his company because they liked him or because they were hoping the friendship would open doors of opportunity, James had soon learned how to read people.

Of course, there were advantages to being Will's son as well. Getting into the business had been easier and having female companions never was a problem, even in his teen years.

James's distinguished good looks were well established by the time he was sixteen. His thick, shiny black hair, tanned skin, dark-brown eyes, and chiseled features were all accredited to his Native American and Scottish ancestry. Even then, his young looks were devastatingly haunting, yet warm and sincere. At least, that was what the magazines said about him. They'd made him sound like the next teen idol.

Unlike Utah, thirty-nine-year-old James still hadn't found the time to settle down. The big 4-0 had come knocking, and he felt anything but.

A smile came to his face as he tuned his guitar, but a shiver passed completely through his six-foot, three-inch body. He passed it off as pre-performance jitters and continued preparing for the night's performance.

James had been informed The Night Ramblers would go on after The Four Guys, making them the fifth act of the night. Showtime was scheduled to begin at nine-thirty, meaning he'd go on somewhere between ten-thirty and eleven o'clock. He prayed everyone was ready to give it their best shot. There'd be no bluegrass coming from his band tonight. Strictly country.

Backup musicians for the Opry took their places on stage in front of the makeshift red barn door. A hush almost like the quiet before the storm fell upon the entire auditorium. Lights slowly dimmed almost to complete darkness. The curtain rose with the lights. A voice on the PA system announced, "Welcome to the Grand Ole Opry!"

So far, Roy Acuff, Jack Green, and Jumpin' Bill Carlisle had played. The group at center stage now were known as The Four Guys. Their style was reminiscent of the Oak Ridge Boys and the Statler Brothers.

"And now, ladies and gentlemen, to sing their new song *Snowy Firelight*, please give a warm welcome to James Sheridan and The Night Ramblers!"

Anticipation and nerves took over James's system. He immediately broke into a cold sweat as he heard his band announced. He felt exuberant, edged with nervous excitement.

James and the boys moved swift and sleek as cats stalking their prey, taking their respective spots on stage. The reception from the audience was tremendous. James could hardly be heard as he began to sing into the microphone.

It's snowing outside tonight
And I'm sittin' alone by the firelight
Sippin' on red rosé wine
Remembering a love that was so fine…

The same feeling of earlier returned. This night was going to bring something into his life that he'd worked so hard for all these years. He didn't know what. Just the feeling that it would as he continued singing his song.

Is he holding you tight
On this snowy night?
Is his love strong
When things go wrong?
Can he make you smile
When the tears begin to fall…

****

A rush of excitement flowed through Heather, sending shivers up her spine. Her hands felt clammy and beads of sweat settled on her brow. She finally understood what Frank had been talking about all these weeks…a feeling few people got to feel.

The audience, too, had been hypnotized by the words and music flowing sweetly and sorrowfully from the band on stage. The singer made her feel every word in her heart and soul.

Suddenly, the same strange sensation built itself up in her again. *Why are the words conjuring up feelings I thought long dead?*

Chapter Five

Last Saturday night at the Opry burned deep in Heather's mind. The bug had really bitten her hard, its essence seeping into her soul.

Heather thought plenty about that night and put to paper the feelings that went through her mind. She smiled as she wrote down her thoughts. How strange and glorious that one night had become the greatest inspiration ever to enter her life.

Rona returned from her weekly trip to the post office waving an envelope in her hand. "Heather, you've got a letter!"

Heather took the envelope and tore it open.

Dear Heather,

It was great hearing from you. Everyone had been asking and were relieved to know that you got a job and all is well.

Ever since you left, I've been doing a lot of thinking. I've come to the conclusion there's nothing to hold me here and if you can start over somewhere else, so can I.

I've given notice here and, with your blessing, would like to join you in Nashville. I've saved up some bucks and two can live as cheaply as one. So what do you say? Think the two of us can take the town by storm? I can be there by next Sunday.

Always,
Kathi

Catching her breath, Heather stared aimlessly as wave after wave of shock bounced against the walls of her mind.

"Heather?"

"It's from a girl I used to work with. Kathi wants to move here…next week." The hesitation wedged in her voice surprised even her. "Kathi's one of the few single friends I had back home. She's already given notice at work and expects to be here by next Sunday. It sounds like a great idea. We could room together and share the expenses." Excitement grew inside her, but the slight touch of disbelief skirted around its edges. "The problem is, where would she stay until we found a place to live? I know it's sudden and…"

"If you don't mind sharing your room, Kathi could stay with us. I mean, how long could it take two determined Yankee women to find an apartment anyway?" Rona handed her the phone. "Go ahead and make the call, Heather."

"Are you sure? What about Robert?" Heather gnawed her bottom lip, worried the offer would be rescinded.

"Robert won't mind. He does love women, after all." Rona laughed as she headed down the hall.

Heather dialed Kathi's office number. It rang about four times before the voice at the other end responded. "Word Processing, Kathi speaking."

"Kathi, it's Heather."

"Heather! Did you get my letter?"

"Yes, that's why I'm calling." Heather tried hard to conceal her excitement. "Pack your bags and get yourself down here, woman."

"Are you kidding?"

"Nope, I'm not kidding. Rona said we both could stay here until we find a place."

"I'll be there sometime next weekend."

****

Snowy Firelight had been a hit the evening The Night Ramblers introduced it at the Opry. The single made the top forty on the country charts and was slowly moving up. One problem—James was still being referred to as "the son of Will Sheridan." That displeased him to no end. Not that he didn't love his father—because he did—he just wanted to do something in this crazy business on his own merit. He'd have to be patient and wait a while longer. Right now, he had to answer the damn phone.

"Hello."

"Is this the residence of James Sheridan?" an unfamiliar, telemarketing-type of male voice inquired.

"Yes, it is." *Whatever you're selling, I'm not buying.*

"Is Mr. Sheridan available?"

"As a matter of fact, you're talkin' to him." *Come on, just get on with it.*

"Oh, hello, Mr. Sheridan. This is Tom Matteson. I'm the campaign manager for Jake Holliday who's running for a senate seat in your district."

"What can I do for you?" *More campaign fund raising no doubt. Once you contribute, they just keep coming back.*

"We're having a fund raiser on Saturday, May 10, and would like you and your band there to perform. Of course, your time would be donated, but we're expecting a big turnout, so the exposure would be good for you.

Besides, with the name of Sheridan backing us, it would be a benefit for our side, as well."

"I don't see any problem, but to make sure, let me check my date book." James got up from his overstuffed easy chair and walked to the big walnut desk. Opening the top drawer, he pulled out his engagement book. *Damn, the date's open! Should I grab the opportunity or lie and turn it down?* He drew in a deep breath knowing lying would get him nowhere. "I was right. That date is open."

"Does that mean you'll do it?"

"It's like you said. It would be to your benefit as well as the group's to do this. As far as I'm concerned, you can count on us being there."

"Okay, it's a deal. I'll get everything in motion. Thanks a lot, Mr. Sheridan."

"Thanks for askin' us. Goodbye." James hung up the phone, thinking about the proposition. God, how he hoped this was a good move, that it wouldn't put him into a stressed situation with his career or jeopardize him and the band in any way. He loved the guys even though they didn't all have the same political views. *A gig is a gig.*

Making his way up the stairs to the master bedroom, he couldn't help but remember all the struggles he'd gone through in his life. How hard he'd worked to get things on his own. It hadn't been easy. There was a lot of sweat, tears, and at least one heartbreak along the way.

The heartbreak had been the hardest of all to overcome. Hard, fast and deep. No better way to describe the way he'd fallen for Suzette Ramsey.

He'd only been twenty years old at the time he was on tour with his father. They were playing at a bluegrass festival in Indiana. The weather had been perfect for the annual outdoor concert, with temperatures in the seventies and no threat of rain in the forecast.

His father's band had been doing their rendition of *Blue Moon of Kentucky* when James first saw her. Her hair shone in the sunlight like spun gold and her eyes were as blue and sparkling as a clear mountain spring. He'd been completely overcome with want and desire the moment their gaze met. She had a smile that could sweeten the sourest piece of candy. It had been love at first sight for James.

A whirlwind romance followed. Suzette traveled everywhere with him. Their love seemed to be complete. Their passion burned brighter, hotter each day they spent together until one day, at a concert, James found a note in his dressing room. It was from Suzette saying, in essence, "Thanks for the ride, time for me to move on."

James had felt as cold as a Midwest winter night inside. Soon after that, he'd written *Snowy Firelight*. Now, after all these years, he finally let that part of his life go public, in his own way. No one, not even his father, knew of the real heartache behind the song.

James stood in his master bedroom, looking out the balcony doors. Dusk was falling, and the lights of the city twinkled in the distance. He watched the lights, briefly wondering where Suzette had gone and what she was doing.

Ever since that day in Louisiana, he'd pledged to devote his time and energy to his career. He hadn't done too badly, either. The nice, comfortable hilltop home he once shared with Utah on the north end of Nashville couldn't be seen from the very public roadway. Thus, privacy.

Now his music career felt as if it was starting to get on track, and all because of a song written out of great pain and sorrow. He hoped those feelings would never be repeated in his lifetime.

Would it be worth it in the end if he were essentially alone? At this time in his life, it was exactly the way he wanted it. He kept women at an emotional distance and his career close at hand.

Chapter Six

Heather had anxiously awaited Kathi's arrival since their phone conversation. Looking all over Nashville for a place to call home, they'd finally found a place just outside the city in Hendersonville and moved in just two weeks ago.

Even though they got along well together, both were relieved their working schedules were different. Kathi worked during the day, giving Heather plenty of time to be alone during sunny days basking in the warmth of the sun or feeding the geese in the park. Each of them maintained a certain amount of privacy while remaining friends.

Heather couldn't be happier with what lady luck had thrown her way over the past several months. If only the luck stayed with her long enough to get some of her material at least considered. She knew the nerve-wracking struggle could be long and hard, but with some determination, a little patience, and a lot of faith, the waiting would one day come to an end. She'd become the accomplished songwriter she longed to be and her most cherished dream would become a reality. The thought of it sent a shiver up her spine.

Heather's thoughts turned to the benefit dinner Frank asked her to accompany him to. This would be no casual affair, so she selected a sweet, innocent, white-lace dress with high-button collar and pleated skirt. She took special care to make sure everything looked right. One never knew whom one might meet at a political social function.

****

Frank stood over the bathroom sink shaving. He couldn't help but think of Heather. He'd been spending a lot of time with her ever since that night weeks ago at the Opry. In fact, some went so far as to consider them an "item."

Imagination and what-ifs took over his sensibilities as those whispered musings captured his mind. Gazing into the mirror, instead of a face full of shaving cream, the reflection of an anxious man fussing over his hair stared back at him. He was clean-shaven and it appeared the makings of a tux graced his shoulders. Stroking his chin with razor in hand, the sudden stinging sensation of the blade snapped him out of his musings.

"Damn!" Frank put the razor down and grabbed a towel to catch the blood seeping out. Chuckling to himself, he looked back into the mirror.

"Well, Frank, my boy, you've finally gone off the deep end!" Wiping the remaining shaving cream off his face, he shook his head.

"You don't even have the nerve to give Heather the kind of kiss your body aches for each time you see her. Better get a hold of yourself, buddy! She's not interested and neither should you be."

Chapter Seven

Heather and Frank arrived at the fundraiser and found the place buzzing with politicians, musicians, businessmen, etc. Locating a table near the bandstand, she watched as he left to get them something to drink then pulled up a chair next to her.

"Seems we got here just in time. The speeches are about to begin, but keep your dance card open. Or at least try to save one for me." There was a twinkle of laughter in his eye as he gave Heather a smile.

"Oh, It seems pretty full already," Heather softly teased. "But, if there's a cancellation, I'll be sure to pencil you in."

The speeches and campaign promises were taking forever. Heather felt restless with the need to move around. She fidgeted, adjusting the hem of her dress constantly.

Frank leaned over, whispering, "What I wouldn't do for some cherry Lifesavers right now." She muffled a chuckle as she pictured him as a child, being given some candy in an attempt to get him to sit still and be quiet. The thought brought warmth to her heart.

Finally, the MC announced the party festivities would begin. Finger food and beverages were ready for those who didn't get enough to eat, and the music would start within a few minutes. The applause clearly signaled gratitude and an eagerness to get on with the last half of the evening.

The toe-tappin' music got everyone on their feet and out on the dance floor. Frank tried to accomplish the impossible by teaching Heather the Texas Two-Step. She laughed at her inability to get the sequence of the steps right, feeling she had two left feet each time she tried to master the dance.

****

Frank wished they'd play a slow dance as the band began playing an Oak Ridge Boy's tune. As the words and melody of *Dream On* floated through the hall, Frank held Heather closer than he'd ever dared before.

The softness of her hair and the warmth of her body next to his filled his senses. The building desire for her within him climbed to a peak, and he gently moved his hand up to her cheek. His trembling fingers lightly touched her skin. Heather looked into his eyes as his lips softly met hers.

For an instant, she responded to the warmth of their kiss, but then the love song faded and she suddenly stiffened. Pulling away from him, she ran out of the hall and onto the balcony overlooking the grounds.

Frank stood on the dance floor ashamed of what he'd done. *Could I possibly be falling in love? How could I let myself get carried away and put that kind of pressure on her?*

****

Heather stood in the shadows, looking out at the clear sky and full moon. She wanted to blend into the darkness. She couldn't bring herself to turn and face Frank. It was impossible to melt away.

"Excuse me, Miss, but are you all right?"

The voice, much deeper with a pure southern accent edged with a soft, masculine ring to it, wasn't Frank's.

"Miss, are you okay?"

She turned and gazed into a pair of concerned chocolate-brown eyes. "Yes," she replied in a trembling small voice.

Frank walked out onto the balcony toward her. The three of them stood in the moonlight, looking at each other, not knowing whether to speak. Finally, the stranger broke the deafening silence.

"Frank, I was looking for you. My drummer, Jordan, can't make it tonight, which leaves me at a great loss. When I saw you dancing, I was hoping you'd be able to fill in for him. But I can see you have other plans, so I'll try to find someone else. It was nice seeing you again." The man turned to leave.

"Wait a minute." Frank turned away from Heather. "You want me to sit in with your band?" The surprise in his voice expressed visible waves of shock flowing through his body.

"Yeah. If I didn't think you could handle it, I wouldn't have asked ya."

"How soon do you need me?"

"In about half an hour. You'll do it?"

"You bet! Just give me a few minutes here, and I'll be right there."

"Okay. And Frank, thanks." With appreciation showing in his eyes, the man left Heather and Frank on the balcony.

"Heather."

He lightly touched her shoulder, and she whirled toward him, tears threatening to fall down her cheeks. "Frank, don't."

As she stood with her back against the railing, the moonlight showed the sorrow and pain on his face. He reminded her of a little boy who'd done something very wrong but didn't realize it until it was too late.

"Heather, please listen. I'm sorry. I wasn't thinking when I…well, you know." With renewed humiliation, he looked away.

In an attempt to ease his embarrassment as well as her own, she walked over to him. "There was a time in my life when I fell deeply and totally in love. The love was never returned. At least…not the way I wanted and needed it then. Anyway, after the relationship had gone on for two years, I found out he was married." Heather turned away. She just couldn't bear for him to see the shame and grief ripping at her heart once again. "I made a promise to never let a man get that close again…physically or emotionally."

Chapter Eight

The weight of the world shifted off Heather's shoulders as she felt Frank's arms around her. Turning, she buried her face into his shoulder. Frank held her gently in his arms, stroking her long hair and letting her weep softly.

After a few minutes, Frank escorted Heather back to their table. "I hate to leave you…"

She sucked in her feelings and put the brightest smile on her face she could muster. "Go," she said, waving him away. "You have an opportunity here, and I'm gonna be fine. Really I am. Go show them how good a drummer you are."

Frank squeezed her shoulder and then all but jogged off. During those moments, her thoughts drifted back to that time when she was younger and so much in love. So totally in love that nothing seemed to be more important.

Josh had been her whole world then.

At a party given by some mutual friends, Heather had had the feeling someone was staring a hole right through her. Her gaze crossed the room and fell upon a man with compelling blue eyes. His hot gaze wouldn't release its hold on her body. By the end of the evening, they were side-by-side feeling a strong want and desire for each other. Heather had fallen in love.

Closing her eyes, she tried to shut off the very feelings she'd promised herself never to let happen again. She'd be the one in control the next time around…if there'd even be a next time.

Music slowly floated around her, chasing away the past and letting in the present. She felt like she was in a dream world. The words of a song that had touched her inner soul a few months before floated around her. Looking in the direction of the melody, her gaze met those of the singer— the same dark, caring eyes that had seen her earlier tears.

A cottony mist surrounded him. His dark, curly hair was mussed, inviting fingers to run through it. The sadness Heather had felt when she first heard the song lingered in his eyes. Intense astonishment touched her.

With guitar in hand stood the very same man that had been a mystery and a cloud of uncertainty. He looked very much like the Prince Charming she'd always dreamt of as a child. *How could I dream of a man I've never seen before? It's not possible.*

She hadn't noticed the music stop. She couldn't take her eyes off the tall, tanned man in the black cowboy hat. Her gaze trailed him to a table where several people, including a pretty little brunette, waited for him. Now she understood why he hadn't given her a second glance. She couldn't compete with the beauty sitting there.

"Hey, are you here or off on some cloud?" Frank sat watching her look across the room at the other band members.

"What?"

Frank sat across from her, drumming his fingers on the table.

The repetitive cadence annoyed her to no end. "Oh. Frank. Yeah, I'm here. Just a little tired, I guess."

"Tell you what, it's been a big night and I'm totally exhausted. Why don't we just head out?"

"That sounds like a good idea." Heather sighed with relief.

She was emotional drained, and annoyed at the emotions traveling through her when she'd met the eyes of the mysteriously attractive lead singer. All she wanted was to be home, safe in bed, and sort out the old and unexpected feelings that had arisen during the course of the evening.

She hoped the rejection of Frank's kiss didn't hurt their friendship. The electricity she'd felt when she looked at that singer would also have to be dealt with. The feeling not only scared her, but it angered her more than anything. The best thing to do would be to push that part of the night completely out of her mind. *Another Josh, I don't need or want right now.*

****

James kept watch from dance floor to the balcony as he helped his crew get the equipment ready for loading on to the truck. The balcony doors stood open. The image of the woman fresh in his mind, he found himself standing outside in the very spot where he'd followed her.

He'd been returning from a phone call when he'd seen her push out of Frank's arms and run toward the balcony. He'd been lying when he said he was looking for Frank; he knew where he was. For some unexplained reason, he'd felt compelled to follow that woman. Before he could stop himself, he'd been standing behind her listening to her sniffle softly.

There was something familiar about being in that spot. Looking in the pond, he'd seen the moonlight reflecting on her hair and the smell of lavender had filled his senses. *Where have I smelled that before?*

As soon as she'd turned with pools of tears in hazel eyes, his heart had gone out to her. Deep pain and sorrow reflected in them. He couldn't help feel those horrible feelings with her. It had unnerved him, as it did now, to think someone he didn't know had, with no effort or knowledge, reminded him of Suzette.

Hands gripping the balcony's stone railing, James stood with tears in his eyes. He looked to the sky, hoping to find in the stars relief and answers to his confusion in the stars, and prayed he wouldn't fall for this woman as he'd done so many years ago for another.

Romance and love. I don't want it. Not now. I have a career to run. I can't tolerate another fly-by-night relationship.

Rain sprinkled on his face and lightning filled the sky. James took a deep breath, sucking in the wind that had kicked up. He turned to go back inside and close the double glass and wooden doors and caught an image of the unhappy woman. As the doors clicked shut, the image disappeared and James went on with his work.

Chapter Nine

Fan Fair—the height of the tourist season for Nashville. The hotel was packed, keeping everyone busy doing double duty not only in the restaurant, but throughout the entire hotel. It had taken Heather a little longer to count the night's receipts and make sure everything was in order for the morning. By the time she arrived at Gabe's Lounge, the parking lot was full and the walls seemed to take on a life of their own.

Frank nodded, flashing his signature smile as she walked into the club. They'd already resolved the misunderstanding of his impromptu kiss of a few weeks ago. No one knew what had happened, and she'd rather keep it that way.

She'd hurt him in denying his romantic ideas, and she was sorry for that. She'd explained that she valued his friendship more than anything, far more than allowing a closeness she couldn't return. It wouldn't be fair to either of them.

As she continued to scan the crowd, her gaze stopped abruptly. Her body trembled in apprehension and excitement.

He's here! The gaze of the man who'd stirred sensual desires in her deep within their long ago dug grave met hers. A soft gasp escaped her. The nod of his head and wink of his eye made her blush. Her heart pounded, trying to escape its chamber.

She studied every inch, every line of his face. Her memory drank in everything about him. Tall, rawboned, beardless, and the most adorable dimples...*sigh*. His black hair gleamed in the bar light, and a swath of curl fell casually across his forehead. His kissable mouth curled as if on the edge of laughter. But his eyes said it all. They filled her with safety and security. She was drawn into their warmth, convinced no harm could come to her.

"Heather, the usual?"

Heather's heart skipped a beat at the sound of Janey's voice. She didn't think she'd been that engrossed in checking out her mystery man.

"I'm sorry, I didn't mean to scare you."

"Hey, that's okay. It's what I get for goo-gooing someone." The music stopped, and she looked for the object of her engrossment. He'd disappeared into thin air. "Yeah, the usual. Brandy Old Fashioned Sour."

Frank sat on the stool next to her, reaching for the beer Janey automatically set down. "Whew! This has been one hell of a night. You must have been just as busy at the hotel." Sweat ran down the side of his face from underneath his hat.

"Hey, Frank!"

Frank took off his hat, shaking his damp hair before running fingers through it. "Yeah?"

"You got a minute? I need to talk some business with you."

Oh my god! He's still here...mere inches from me. Don't look like some star-eyed puppy dog now. You're a grown woman, not a love-struck teenager. Heather took a long sip of her drink through the straw, nearly emptying the tumbler. The liquid warmth spread through her like fire threatening out of control.

"I've got about ten minutes. Let's go outside so we don't have to shout." Frank grabbed his beer and the two men walked out through the back door.

Heather admired the sway of a pair of butts that would be a match for any ranch cowboy. She couldn't believe one person could disappear and reappear as if by magic. *I have to find out more about that guy.*

****

The night air carried the lingering warmth of the day's sun. The patio tables were empty, so James claimed one in the farthest corner from the door and the club.

"Well, James, whaddya need?" Frank took a swig of his beer, eyeing James with suspicion.

"I wanted to thank you for helping me out at the gig a few weeks ago. You did a great job picking up on our style of music." James knew Frank was getting nervous; he kept looking back to the door leading inside the club. *Probably worried about his lady waiting inside.* James had asked around about the woman, and the general consensus was she and Frank were a number.

Taking a drink of his draft beer, he wondered whether things would go as he hoped. *Come on, man, ask him.* "The fact is Jordan is leaving. I'm asking you to fill in until a suitable replacement can be found. I realize you have a club to worry about, but I'm sure your partners can handle things while you're away. The question is, if you're interested, can you get away from Shadow Records?"

Frank's eyes glazed over and he sat back in his seat. For several moments, he looked into the darkening sky. "I'll take a leave from Shadow for a bit, and my partners would love to have me out of here for a while."

He stretched his hand out to James and the two shook hands. "Son, you've got yourself a new drummer. Now, how about a shot of Jack to celebrate?"

Frank got up and jogged into club for their poison. Now that the easy part was taken care of, James searched his mind to find a way of getting more information about the lady Frank had been rumored to be spending a lot of time with.

Frank stepped back through the patio doors, shot glasses and bottle of Jack Daniels in hand.

"What should we toast to?" Frank sat then poured the amber liquid into each glass. "I know. How about success, wine, and…women?"

James raised his shot glass, meeting Frank's halfway. He swallowed the liquor, feeling the warmth travel down his throat and heat his stomach at the end of its journey. Waiting for the whiskey to settle, he held the draft, thanking Frank for the opening he needed.

Taking a long draw of the beer, the tension and nervousness eased slightly. "Women? I'm surprised you'd drink to women since you've got such a beautiful one waiting for you inside." The quaver in his voice took him by surprise. James was a man known for his composure, but anyone who knew him wouldn't think so of him now.

"Who are you takin' about?" Frank laughed, slapping his cowboy hat on the table. "You mean Heather? She's not my woman. In fact, she's not anyone's woman."

"You mean the two of you aren't…?"

"Nope, just close friends." Frank poured them each another two fingers of whiskey, "When she came here, I was one of the first people she met. Robert asked me to…well…sort of watch after her a few times. At least until she got to know a few more people."

James downed the whiskey and followed it with another swig of beer. "Does she know that?"

"Are you kidding? If she ever knew, she'd have a hissy fit. Heather's the type of woman who likes to be self-functional. Doesn't want to depend on anyone, although I think deep down inside, she needs to."

"Mmmm, and no one's asked her out yet?" James drummed his fingers on the table, a nervous habit he'd yet to kick.

"I suppose because people are under the illusion we're an item. A few have expressed interest, but she stays cool and distant."

"A cold fish then." *Great, I had to pick a woman who didn't warm up. Just what I get for thinking I could get to know her.*

"She got hurt bad one time and won't venture down that path again." Frank downed the rest of his beer, thumping the empty bottle on the table. "If you remember right, I found that out not too long ago."

James nodded, recalling the kiss that didn't make the cut. Suspicion raced through his mind. It had been too easy finding out about her. Because of Frank, he knew her name and a bit more about her personality. Granted, he usually fell for women who were anything but the strong and silent type.

Obviously, Frank had feelings for Heather. The tone of his voice and the flash in his eyes signaled that much. James suspected the incident of a few weeks ago had something to do with their not-too-mutual feelings. Frank must want more, but settled for friendship. So, this was the type of woman who needed to be handled carefully, without pushing.

****

Heather stood at the patio doors, watching Frank and his friend finish off the bottle of Jack Daniels. She didn't know about the other man, but Frank wasn't going to be in any shape to drive home tonight. She'd have to talk to Janey and see who could take him home.

She pushed open the sliding doors and walked out into the night, straight for the table.

"Heather!" Frank's slightly slurred voice wafted through the night. "You'll never guess. James here has offered me a job. Isn't that great?" His exuberance had no difficulty getting past the whiskey in his system.

Heather picked the bottle off the table, looking at James and then Frank. "What are you talkin' about? I think your friend Jack has been paying you an extended visit, Frank." Flashing him a look of disdain, she sat and waited for an explanation. She had a feeling once morning came, Frank's dream world would evaporate.

"I haven't had as much as you think. Just listen to me. James…" Frank motioned to James, who'd been sitting quietly since she'd stepped out on to the deck, "offered to bring me on as the band's new drummer."

James smiled at her, obviously enjoying Frank and his condition and her feelings about it. "That's right. He did a good job at that political function. So when an opening popped up, Frank came to mind." His voice showed hardly any indication of the whiskey. His words were so smooth, the huskiness seemed to soften with each word. "So, you see he's not, as you put it, 'talkin' through his head.'"

Smart ass. Why do men think they can talk like that to a woman, anyway? "What about the club, Frank? Who's going to take care of it? Not to mention Shadow Records."

Frank sat back in his chair, obviously confused by her reaction. "I have two other partners, and I could use the break. Anyway, let's celebrate by going to *Tommy's* at bar time."

Heather grabbed the almost-empty whiskey bottle. "At least you'll have time to sober up a little." Stepping away from the table, she stopped within a few feet of the patio door. She turned to find both men staring at her with two completely different expressions.

One of drunken gaiety.

One of smugness.

Chapter Ten

Heather couldn't believe the man behind the wheel of the car. She'd seen that look he'd flashed her a few hours ago and the glint that followed quickly afterward. She'd never really understood why men looked at her as if they were undressing her.

Although she was in shape, her body was of the typical female proportions. As far as she was concerned, she looked like any other Midwestern woman. But when a man gave her a lustful look and invaded her privacy without seeming to really care, it upset her and made her feel cheap. She just couldn't figure out what the big deal was.

Heather sat in the back seat of the car trying to hear what the guys were talking about. She was happy for Frank, truly, but upset at the same time. She was unsure whether guilt had put her in the car, or the unwanted building desire to be near James.

What is it with men and whiskey? I can't let jealousy get in the way of our friendship, or allow his friend to push me aside, either.

I can't let Frank down and not join in his celebration. He'd share in her happiness she was sure of it. That was it…wasn't it? *God, I don't know. Something, no make that someone, inside pulled me into this car.*

It annoyed her that he'd been able to unearth long ago forgotten desires and passions.

I can't let James's smooth moves get to me. I can't afford to fall into the depths of his eyes or allow him into my soul. She shivered at the thought. She'd been so careful since Josh. Just who was she more upset with? James? Or herself?

"We're at *Tommy's*, and so is everyone else, it would seem." Frank jumped out of the car and then held the seat up and door open for Heather.

She placed a foot outside the door as a hand reached out in an effort to help. The large hand with long, strong fingers pulled her gently from the back seat of the Mark IV. Her gaze locked on to a face that didn't belong to Frank. A spark of electricity shot right through her as James's returned gaze plugged into hers.

****

"Where's Frank?" Heather asked, trying hard to conceal the current giving a warm glow off her cheeks. The sentiment sent a wave of heat through James. He looked away, not breaking the connection between them.

"Over there," James said, pointing toward a grey Ford van. He felt the need to pull Heather close to him, but he was a gentleman. *She's just another female.* "As soon as the guys pulled up, he was off. I guess you're stuck with me as your escort inside."

Fighting to conceal his smoldering desire for her, James took Heather by the elbow, directing her to the line at the front door. "He'll find his way, don't worry."

"So many people trying to fit into one area?" Wonderment edged her voice and she clung closer to him, igniting a desire to protect her.

"The place is bigger than it looks. It used to be an old office building. The walls on the top floor were gutted to make room for a stage, tables and chairs, and the usual bar activities. You'll be surprised by its size."

"Well, James. How ya doin' buddy?"

"Just fine, Bubba," James accepted the outstretched hand, acknowledging the greeting. He strolled through the door and up the stairs with Heather in tow. She lagged just a bit, but he kept pace up to the top.

"Bubba?" Heather's voice reflected her amusement.

"Bubba." James chuckled. "Don't worry, he's just a big ol' pussy cat."

Reaching the top of the stairs, James smiled as Heather turned back to take another look at the bouncer.

"Yo, James!" A trio of male voices sang out in unison from a table near the front. Ron, Duwayne, and Frank stood there waving their arms and yelling at them like *The Three Stooges* in one of their black-and-white films.

James waived, tightening his grip on Heather's arm.

****

A chill ran up Heather's spine. It felt as if every eye in the place was on her and James. *Quit being so damn paranoid and enjoy yourself.* She drew in a calming breath.

Reaching Frank, she threw her arms around his neck. "Frank, I'm so sorry about that scene earlier tonight. I guess I'm a wee bit jealous and a tad too protective. Please forgive me." Releasing her hold on him, she looked him straight in the eye. If he didn't forgive her, she'd die right there in a heap of nothing on the floor. She needed someone she trusted in her personal space.

"You nit, I forgive you." Frank hugged her back, giving her his best brotherly kiss on the cheek. "Let's party. Dance a lot. Drink a little. Just have a generally wild time."

31

She nodded, relieved. Tonight would be one of the many bumps in the road yet to come her way in this business and the people she surrounded herself with. She had so much to learn about the music business. *Please give me patience when I need it most*, she silently prayed.

James returned from the bar with a bottle of champagne and five glasses. He placed a glass in front of each of them and began to pour.

"I'd like to make a toast," he shouted loud enough to be heard above the band. "To Frank, and the talent which brought him to my band."

"Here, here." Five glasses rose and clicked together.

"Wait, I have one more toast." Frank turned, looking down at Heather. "To a beautiful lady who has touched our lives. May she find the happiness she seeks and desires."

"Here, here."

Heather felt her cheeks warm with embarrassment. She looked up at Frank and mouthed "Thank you" as she joined in with the others.

Chapter Eleven

Music flowed and the crowd grew thicker as the night wore on. The dance floor was crowded. Heather danced whenever the band played a slow song.

James was the only one she had yet to dance with. Being in a small group with him gave her an uneasy feeling. She gathered her purse to go to the powder room. She hoped the few quieter moments to think and sort things out ease her mind. Getting directions, Heather pushed her way through the crowd and into the restroom.

She stood in front of the mirror, taking a moment to catch her breath. Her thoughts wandered back to the night of the Opry and the hauntingly beautiful love song that had moved her heart.

Startled by two girls bounding into the room, she fumbled around in her purse. She felt them stare and heard their whispers. Were they directed at her? Or was it her imagination running amuck again?

"Is that her?"

"Yeah. How'd she manage to get with him, anyway?"

"I don't know, but she's a new one."

Deciding she'd heard enough, Heather left the girls with their gossip. *Why did that damn song pop into my head? Why were those two girls whispering about me and whoever?* These questions could easily be dismissed, but the feeling she got when she was around James couldn't.

Damn him. Damn him for having the power to reach deep down into my soul and stir up passions I thought were buried. Shit, I let my guard down. Damn him! Heather scolded herself for the umpteenth time as if she needed continuous reminders of the heartbreak men cause.

When she finally returned to the table, James was alone waiting. Her nerves crackled as if their circuits were damaged.

"Heather?"

"Yes?" she asked, trying to deny the pulsing knot forming in her throat.

Before she could find out what he wanted, the lead vocals of the band drew her attention.

"As is customary here at Tommy's, we have a guest musician sit in with us. Tonight is no different." Looking toward them, the singer pointed, and a blinding light lit up their faces. "James, would you honor us with a song?"

James smiled and waved. Thankfully, the hot, white light followed him as he made his way up to the stage. Turning, he said something to the band members as he strapped on a borrowed guitar.

"I'd like to dedicate this song to everyone who's ever been in love and lost." With guitar in hand, James began to sing the song that had invaded Heather's mind just moments earlier.

Heather's heart jolted and her pulse pounded. The song that touched her heart belonged to him. She didn't want to believe a song so beautiful could belong to James; her mind wouldn't accept what her heart knew.

No, it has to be a coincidence.

The pain and sorrow she'd heard in his voice could also be seen in his eyes—the same dark eyes that had tried to sooth her one starry night. She listened as James sang a song of lost love. A hazy light enveloped his face and body. A quiver surged through her veins. Barely able to control the gasp of surprise, her heart knew for sure that James was the man in her dreams, standing exactly the same.

No, my mind's playing tricks on me. Could he really be my dream man?

Struggling to get a hold on herself, Heather shook her head hoping to clear it of the confusion. By the time the song ended, Heather saw James as he'd been before the haze.

****

James left the stage in a round of applause. The house band was already back to business before he'd reached the table. The hair on his arms stood straight up and a chill ran through his body, as if someone was staring a hole through him. When he turned toward Heather, the chill intensified.

He'd been trying to get the nerve to ask her to dance all night. Just as he was about to, he was called up to play with the band. The timing couldn't have been more off. Now, with the music switched to a slower pace, he knew it was now or never.

"Heather?" He stood next to her, his hand extended. "Would you like to dance?"

She placed her hand in his, allowing him to lead her to the dance floor.

The Rose was being sung as a vague sensuous light passed between them. Her warmth seeped into him, encouraging his heart to race faster. A delicate thread formed, sewing their bodies closer and closer.

Heather looked up at him, her eyes never leaving his for an instant. She was delicious in his arms; she fit him perfectly. Dark inner feelings surfaced, intensifying as the song came to an agonizing end. Not wanting to let her to slip away, he devoured her soft mouth with his own in a long, smoldering kiss.

She quivered against him and then she was gone, leaving behind a cold, empty space.

How could you allow a Yankee woman to cast a spell on you?

He'd been fighting a burning desire to kiss her for weeks, ever since that night on the balcony. The tears in her hazel eyes had looked like pools of water in the moonlight. He admitted to himself that he'd lost himself to her then. Unable to cope with her closeness a moment longer, he set out for a good, stiff shot of anything.

****

The smoldering heat from their kiss still on her lips, Heather was grateful James didn't return to the table. This man had stolen the key to her locked passion. She'd fallen under his spell and hadn't tried to stop it.

How? When did he cast his southern charm on me? Why didn't I stop it?

She knew the answer—because it felt so wonderful, so pleasurable to be in his arms, if only once.

She'd have to make sure it didn't happen again. Close the door and lock it—only this time, hold on to the key, keep a tight hold of it, and concentrate on her career. All she had to do was stay out of James's arms.

"I see you fell into James's clutches out there." Heather recognized Frank's slurred voice. "He's been askin' about you lately." His alcohol-glazed eyes looked into Heather's, revealing a hint of concern and something resembling jealousy.

"You know, if one of you three had been around, I wouldn't have had to dance with him," Heather bit back, unfairly blaming them for what happened.

"Hey, now, wait a darn minute here," Lee defended. "I, for one, don't like being blamed for you not being able to say 'no' to him. It would have done him a world of good not getting his way for once."

"What do you mean by that?" she asked, hurt by the accusation no matter how true his words were. "Are you saying that I can't say 'no' to anyone? I wanted to dance, not just sit here. He happened to ask. That's all!"

"Hon, no one's saying that 'bout you. It's just that James has women standing in line all the time. He's never been told no before." Ron gave her a hug, followed by a brotherly kiss.

"You know that we're all very protective of you. We just don't want you to get caught in his trap." Frank's eyes pleaded with her through their glassiness. It was a wonder he could see, let alone talk or think. "Please don't be upset with us. James is a good guy, fun to be around and a great musician. His track record with the ladies is questionable, to say the least."

Heather took a sip from her fresh glass of wine. *Boy, do I need this. What the hell is going on with these three anyway? If I didn't know better, I'd think they were jealous. Men! Who needs 'em?*

"So tell me, what's the big deal? He just asked me to dance." Heather sighed, waiting to hear what three liquor-fogged minds came up with.

The three men exchanged glances until Frank finally spoke up. "You don't know who he is, do you?"

"Yes, I do. He's James and a musician, so what? He's not any different than the three of you in that aspect."

"James Sheridan." The name rang out in harmony, as if she should recognize it.

"So, big deal." Heather felt more confused than ever. "I don't understand. Is his name supposed to mean something to me?"

Frank sat down next to her, placing a hand on her shoulder. "Heather, honey. It seems you've been captivated by the son of Will Sheridan."

She knew full well who Will Sheridan was. She couldn't comprehend how James could be his son. Their music was totally different; some would say opposite ends of the totem pole. Thinking back to the girls in the ladies room, she knew they'd been talking about him…and her.

Another notch, huh? We'll see about that. No one's going to add me to his list of women!

Her guard flew up and the doors to her heart slammed shut, echoing as if they were doors in a long, empty castle hall. She'd wanted to learn about James, but this? This was too much for her to handle. She emptied her glass of wine in one long gulp.

Chapter Twelve

"Let's get out of here. It's almost dawn, and I'd like to get some sleep." James put his hand on Frank's shoulder.

"Yeah, I think Heather's pretty tired." Judging from the look in Heather's drooping eyes, Frank knew it was much more than that. A trace of shock lingered on her face matched with bewilderment. He was sorry he'd even opened his mouth about James. *Too damn honest for my own good. Too damn much drink and too stupid to keep my mouth shut!*

"Let's hit the road."

Frank took Heather by the elbow, leading her towards the door. The awakening morning licked their faces. He slipped his arm around her shoulder. He guessed she couldn't make heads or tails out of what happened tonight. Once she got some sleep, he hoped her mind would be clearer and she'd understand what they'd done…and forgive them for their stupidity.

Before sliding into the front seat, Frank whispered, "Don't worry, Heather. It'll be okay."

James got behind the wheel, started the car, and headed for the other side of town. "Heather, where do you live?"

"Hendersonville on Hunter's Trail," she answered, her words barely audible.

"I can show you," Frank replied, noting the puzzled look on James's face. "I think our little Yankee had too much wine for one night."

"I think we've all had too much wine and excitement for a night or two." James turned on to the freeway heading north onto Interstate 65. By the time they'd reached Two Mile Parkway, the sun had risen and the city showed signs of waking up. "We've got to hit the road in about two months, Frank. That enough time for you to tie up some loose ends and make some business arrangements?"

Frank watched James adjust and gaze into his mirror. "Plenty of time."

If he'd known revealing James's true identity would've affected Heather the way it did, he never would've said anything. If they hadn't been drinking, he would've left well enough alone. She would have found out the right way and by the right person—James.

They pulled out onto Gallatin Road and Frank looked out his window. "She had no idea who you were until three drunken fools decided to inform her. Your reputation reaches most women before you do and, well, we thought..."

They closed in on the Hendersonville city limits and James glanced in the rear view mirror again. "I know she didn't know who I was. Let me tell you about that night of Holiday's function. I went to the balcony looking for you when I heard soft sobbing. I reached out to see if the lady was all right when she turned, her eyes filled with tears." James turned left onto Hunter's Trail. "Call me crazy, but I felt something in those eyes. A pain and sorrow I was sure only I'd ever experienced."

"Her place is just around the bend. First duplex on your right, just over the bridge, second driveway." Frank reached into the back seat, gently shaking Heather's arm. "Heather, honey. You're home."

The car pulled up to the kitchen door as Heather opened her eyes. She smiled sleepily at Frank, then stretched her arms until her hands touched the inside roof of the car. Frank opened the door and helped Heather out from the back seat.

"Thanks for the ride home." Taking Frank's hand, she gave it an extra squeeze. "Can you bring my car back to me around 3:30? I have to be at work by 4:00."

"No problem. Get some sleep; we'll talk then."

"Thanks. 'Night, Frank." Heather put her key into the lock and then turned and opened the deadbolt. When it clicked to its locking position and she was safely behind the closed door, they left.

****

James headed the Mark IV out of Hendersonville into the morning traffic. Deciding to avoid the morning rush, he took Dickerson Road back to Gabe's.

Heather baffled him. Why would knowing who he was, or rather who his father was, upset her? She didn't seem the type to believe in rumors. Then again, the news came from a person she trusted...and that person wasn't him. He had to make things right. She deserved so much more.

"Frank, can I get Heather's phone number from you?" he asked with hesitation.

"Why?"

"I'd like to find out why she's so upset, for one thing. Try to straighten things out about me."

"Why? Isn't she just another female?"

"Another female! Are you kidding? She's…well, she's…" *What the hell are you so afraid of? You can't even tell her she's not just another woman to go out with. You know damn well she's the type of woman you'd take home.*

Frank chuckled, and then slapped James on the shoulder. "You're really attracted to her, aren't you? Get in line, buddy, 'cause you ain't the only rooster after that chicken."

"I'd like to find out why it bothers her who my family is." James took a right onto Trinity Lane, swallowing the information Frank so graciously fed him. *So, I'm not the only one that wants to court her.*

"Man. Okay, I'll give it to you. But you have to give her a few days to get things in her head straightened out."

James turned onto Artic Avenue and into the parking lot of Gabe's. "Thanks, even if it is against your better judgment."

Frank shook his head. "You've no idea. Got a pen and something to write on?"

"Glove box."

Frank popped open the compartment and found what he needed. "Remember, give her a couple of days before you try calling her." He handed the paper over to James and hopped out of the car.

James rolled down the window, calling out to Frank. "See you at six o'clock tonight for a two-hour jam session."

Frank waved as James pulled out of the parking lot, his window still down. The sound of the gravel crunching under the wheels of the car mixed with the song of morning birds.

Chapter Thirteen

Heather woke that afternoon, a slight headache threatening to emerge. She wobbled into the bathroom, ran the bathwater, and popped a couple of aspirins into her mouth. As the hot bathwater steamed up the mirror, she hoped the soak would melt away last night's events swimming around in her head.

Why in the hell did I react like that about James? He didn't pick his parents; it's not his fault he's the son of a world famous musician. She'd never judged anyone until she'd gotten to know them before, why now? "What's done is done. Nothing I can do about it now."

Nothing except apologize and try to explain to James the next time she saw him, if there even was a next time. "What if he doesn't speak to me again? Damn it all!"

Sighing, she slid down into the tub, hot, bubbly water enveloping her, keeping her safe and warm. Just as she'd felt in James' arms last night. Smiling, she closed her eyes, letting the smell of lavender ease her troubled mind.

The sound of tires crunching on the gravel driveway alerted her that her time was up. Fortunately, her little half-hour of luxury had given her body the revitalization it so badly needed after a night of dancing and drinking. She felt like she could take on a whole herd of tourists and their antics.

Heather flew out the kitchen door and jumped into the passenger side of her blue Vega. "Hey, Frank."

"You look a lot better than you did a few hours ago," he said, a smirk on his face.

"I see you haven't shaved yet." Breaking out in laughter, Frank backed the car up and headed toward Nashville.

It was a beautiful late June afternoon. The sky was clear blue and the sun, blazing orange; it was the type of day that made Heather forget that snow and temperatures below zero ever existed.

"Frank?"

"Yeah?"

"I'm really sorry about last night. You know I don't usually behave that way."

"Forget it. What I don't understand is why you got so uptight about James. You two seemed to hit it off. Was it what me and the boys told you?"

"Partly." Sighing, Heather looked down at her hands. "I really am attracted to him, but after what I heard in the bathroom about being on someone's string of women, well, I just got upset when I thought I realized who those girls were talking about. I don't want to be another notch, that's all."

"A what? Listen, all the women James has ever been with have all been after one thing—his money and all that goes with it. They picked him, not the other way around. He knows you're not like that…money hungry. Give it time, Heather, you'll see it'll be just fine." Frank pulled the car into the hotel parking lot, shifted it to park, and looked her straight in the eye. "And since when do you judge a person on hearsay?"

Heather reached for her keys, avoiding the accusing look on Frank's face. "I've got to go in. If they don't work me to death, I'll see you later."

"Okay, subject dropped for now."

She headed inside while Frank dodged around the side, heading to the back and Gabe's.

Heather scampered across the lobby floor. Eyeing the line already forming for dinner, she knew she'd have her work cut out for her tonight. As she reached for the rope closing off the dining room, she saw the beautiful vase of long-stemmed red roses. She paused long enough to take in their wonderful fragrance and then continued into the kitchen.

Snitching a piece of warm apple pie, she got her hand slapped gently before she could stick a fork into it.

"Girl, you're gonna get fat," Annie, the night cook warned, giving Heather another swat that missed by less than an inch.

"But it's soooo good." Heather brought the fork to her mouth, devouring the piece resting on it. "Everything ready for tonight?"

"As ready as can be," purred Shelly. The young and curvy waitress had hopes of finding a sugar daddy. "Napkins are folded, tables set, and candles lit."

"Who sent you the flowers this time, Shelly?" Heather asked, swallowing the last bit of her pie. Shelly was a favorite waitress.

"Sorry, not mine." Shelly smiled and scooted around her.

"Annie, did you and Burt get into a scrap?"

"Honey child, you best go look for yourself. They got here around noon today." Annie smiled and then waddled back into the kitchen.

Heather pushed through the swinging doors and back to the cash register. Smelling the roses again, she found the card and opened it. No message. Just a single name...*James.*

Electricity shot through her body as she read his name a second time. She felt a smile cross her lips as a small buzzer went off signaling dinnertime. Putting the card back into its envelope, she unlatched the rope and began seating hungry tourists.

The aroma from the flowers filled every inch of the dining room. Heather couldn't think of a viable reason why James would send her flowers. She couldn't keep track of how many times she'd been asked who they were from, or how many times she'd simply said "a friend." *One bouquet of flowers doesn't make a lasting relationship, let alone the start of a new one. Whatever the reason, it was a nice gesture.*

Leaving the roses on the counter, she closed up and headed over to meet up with Kathi at Gabe's.

****

As soon as Heather walked through the doors of Gabe's, she heard her name. Spotting Kathi, she pulled out a chair and waited for Brenda to bring her beer.

"How long have you been here?" Heather asked, thanking Brenda for the beer with a good tip.

"Not long, but it seems like hours." Kathi looked unsure of what to do next. "I was lucky to get this table; the place was packed when I got here. I had to stand for a few minutes until some people left, and here we are."

"Have you met anyone yet?" Heather scanned the crowd with secret hopes of seeing James.

"No, but Rona's here. She wants to talk to you." Kathi glanced up as a shadow passed across their table. "Speak of the devil."

"Heather..."

"Well, cousin dear, are you going to tell me, or do I have to beg?" Rona's voice carried a mocking tone with an edge of humor.

Heather looked at her cousin, almost laughing at the look on her face. "Tell you what?" She knew perfectly what; she just wanted to hear Rona ask about the delivery she'd received today.

"Tell me what," Rona murmured under her breath, bringing a smile to Kathi's face. "You know darn well. The flowers. Red roses. Who sent them to you?"

"Oh. The flowers." Heather looked Rona in the eye, hoping the name wasn't written all over her face. "A friend."

"A friend? What friend? Frank?" Rona asked relentlessly.

The music came to a stop, followed by bustling from the stage. Relief flooded her as Frank headed toward their table, giving her a break from

Rona's questions. "No, a new friend."

"Hey Yank, how ya doin'?" Frank leaned down and gave Heather a peck on the forehead. "Rona, how are you? And who is this?" His gaze rested on Kathi's face.

"This is my friend, Kathi Nielson. Kathi, this is Frank Whitman. One of his many talents is being a co-owner of Gabe's."

"Hi." Kathi returned Frank's gaze.

"Are you visiting Heather for a while?" Frank asked, pulling up a chair between Heather and Kathi. If body language was a true indication of a person's thoughts, then Frank was definitely interested in Kathi.

Rona put her hand on Frank's shoulder. "What rock have you been living under? She moved here several months ago. She's Heather's roommate."

"Well, it's about time Heather let you out of the house," he replied in mocked seriousness. "And into the outside world."

The conversation continued until Frank returned to his place under the lights and behind the drums. Kathi and Rona asked each other about work and how living in Nashville was a big change. Heather thought about her lovely roses and the man who sent them.

Will I hear from him again?

The roses seemed to say she would, but common sense indicated not to count on it. What did they really have in common, anyway? He came from a wealthy background, not a middle-class family like hers. She'd already made up her mind not to take any calls from him. That is, if he ever did call, which, of course, he wouldn't.

"Heather, didn't you tell Frank about Kathi?" Rona's voice snapped Heather's mind back to the present and out of the daydream. "He acted like he didn't know about her."

"I think I might have mentioned it. You know Frank. He's had a lot on his mind lately with getting ready for the road and taking care of business here. She shrugged her shoulders and took a drink of her beer. "This is the first time Kathi and I have been out together since she got settled in."

"That's true. Between our alternate schedules, we never have the opportunity. I wanted a few weeks to get started before going headfirst into a new night life." Kathi leaned into Heather, her voice softer. "He's pretty cute. Frank, I mean. Seems awfully nice, too."

"Are we smitten by ole Frank here?" Heather teased, swishing her beer.

Kathi's cheeks turned a pretty shade of pink. "He's just nice and polite, that's all." She took a drink, avoiding Heather's and Rona's eyes.

"Ah-ha." Heather and Rona's voices rang out in unison, giving Kathi a teasing nudge and friendly laugh.

****

Frank made his way back to the girls. The band still played, only behind the skins sat another drummer. He was about to take full advantage of an opportunity to rest and talk with Heather…and her sexy, interesting friend, Kathi.

"Boy, this been a long night." He sat at the table and wiped the sweat off his brow. "James had a practice session all afternoon to 8:30 tonight. We're going out on the road a lot sooner than he initially thought."

"How soon is sooner?" Heather asked, responding to the hint of hesitation flittering across Frank's face. "Do you think you'll be ready?"

"About a month, I guess." Frank took a swallow from the longneck bottle Brenda placed in front of him. "He's made some earlier dates. Ever since that song of his made the Top 40 on the country charts, the offers have been rollin' in. It'll take some getting used to, but I'll survive."

"He couldn't have a better drummer in my opinion." Kathi smiled shyly.

"Thanks, Kathi. Hope you're right." Frank smiled back. "Heather, remember that poem you gave me? Is it mine to do with as I please?"

Heather felt her heart drop. "Of course. Why? You gonna throw it away or something?"

"Or something." Frank looked around and then stood up. "I'd better mingle. Have to keep the customers happy, you know. Rona, nice to see you again. Kathi, be sure to come out again soon." Turning to leave, he paused next to Heather. "Talk to ya later, Yank." He gave Kathi a tip of his hat before moving through the crowd to another table.

Heather watched Frank turn on his charm with a table of tourists. It wouldn't be long and he'd be on the road, unable to mix with the customers so freely. Her thoughts turned back a few pages and she wondered what he wanted to do with her special poem. She'd given it to him, giving up all claims whatsoever to it. She didn't know why, but the feeling he was up to something lingered in the back of her mind.

Chapter Fourteen

Fan Fair hit the middle of its annual weeklong celebration. Totally exhausted by the end of each day, Heather hadn't possessed the ambition to go anywhere except home and straight to bed. Over the last few days, she'd dealt with some pretty rude and unpleasant people. She did her best to keep everyone happy. There was a tally in the restaurant keeping count of how many days were left until Saturday, when the city returned to its normal tourist season.

Kathi, on the other hand, was spending her nights at Gabe's. Heather suspected Frank's presence had a little to do with that. It made her happy two of her friends liked each other so well.

Heather didn't want to think about them or anyone else at the moment, though. She curled up on the couch, turned on TCM, and fell asleep watching *Topper*.

****

The door slammed and she jumped out of her skin as Kathi came bounding in from the kitchen.

"Shit, Kathi. You scared the daylights out of me!" She held her hand to her chest, feeling her heart beat fast.

"Heather, sorry I woke you," Kathi said, gasping for air. "There was a guy asking Frank about you tonight."

"A guy?" Heather sat up, waiting as Kathi caught her breath. "What guy?"

"I think Frank said it was his boss. James, is that his name?" Kathi plopped down on the cushion next to Heather. "They were talking kind of low, but I heard enough to know he wanted to know about you. I thought Frank was a boss. How can James be his boss when—"

"What did this guy look like?" Heather's heart leapt against her chest.

"Tall, dark, and gorgeous. He seemed very anxious about you, like

I said. You'd have to ask Frank for the details. I didn't catch any of that."

"Sounds like James. But it doesn't matter to me in the least." Heather got off the sofa and walked toward the bay window. "You'd better get some sleep."

"You're right. Seven a.m. comes pretty quick." Stretching, Kathi yawned then headed up the stairs to her room. "'Night."

"'Night." Heather peeked out of the drapes. *So, he was asking questions. Whatever he wanted doesn't really matter. Why would he be interested in small-town like me to begin with?* Heather took a deep breath to calm her still-racing heart. She ran her sweaty hands down her jeans.

She let the curtain fall into place and turned off the light. She climbed the stairs to her room, then nestled herself under the blanket. She drifted off to sleep with the haunting stanzas of James's love song. As they had for many nights, the lyrics caressed her into the warm and safe dream world of a tall, dark man.

****

Heather was happy when Sunday night finally arrived and they could all go back to a regular schedule. She finally had time to take a breather and start cleaning up the clutter that had gathered all week. The first item…the wilted roses.

They'd been well past their prime for a few days. She hated throwing them out even if she knew it had to be done. Cutting a single dried bud off, she dropped the rest into the wastebasket. She brought the discolored flower to her nose, hoping to find a lingering scent.

Memories flooded her mind, pushing every other thought aside. She reached for a blank order slip, placed the bud on it, and began to put to paper the wave of feelings flowing through her mind.

I've been sittin' here on this bar stool
With nothin' on my mind but you
Such a proud man
So sure of yourself and everything you do
I remember the night we met
The first time I saw you I was lost in the warmth of your eyes
Your smile seemed to say that you knew we would meet
I was shy at first and unsure of everything I saw in your face
We danced and took a walk in the moonlight
Our love so fresh and young
It was as if we had our own world
A few days have gone by now
I'm wonderin' if we'll have the time to go back and do it all again
I believe we will as long as you stay on my mind.

The words flowed easily through the pen in her hand. It had been a long time since anything creative had flowed out of her mind. Heather folded the paper in half, placing the browned rose bud near the crease. She carefully placed it inside her purse before continuing the work at hand, wondering if she believed her own words.

****

The club had been very busy the past week. On top of that, rehearsals with The Night Ramblers were heating up. With the winding down of Fan Fair, James pushed all the guys hard and Frank felt its effects. He was worn out, but welcomed the mounting excitement as his first major road trip approached.

Keeping low-key, Frank found sanctuary in fitting a melody to Heather's poem. Each night, he'd sat behind the piano to work on it after closing. He hoped she wouldn't disapprove of him doing it. He was bound and determined to give her a quiet little push in the right direction.

He didn't feel she'd been pushing hard enough for her dream, if at all. Maybe if he played this song some night, she'd realize her potential and really start to contact some people. He'd have to get the melody down and then introduce it at the club. Hell, he'd bring in one of the execs from Shadow Records. No harm in that, was there?

Frank concentrated on the ivory and the melody. His fingers hitting a series of keys, he picked up a pencil and transferred the notes onto paper. He paused for a moment, pondering the next melody sequence.

"A beer. I need a beer." Frank stood, stretching his fingers. "No, a cola would be better." Turning, he saw James sitting at the bar.

"Hey, buddy." Frank sauntered over to the bar, trying not to act as nervous as he felt. "When did you come in?" His eyes connected with James's and he wondered just how much James had heard.

"A few minutes ago." James stepped over to the piano, picking up the piece of sheet music with Frank's scratching on it. "What's this? You were so engrossed in it I didn't want to disturb your creative thought process."

Shit! "Want a cola?" Frank didn't wait for James's answer and poured them both a tall glass. He handed James one and reached out for the sheet music, his hands trembling. James was the last person he expected to see mid-afternoon.

"Nothin', really." Frank put the paper into its folder then closed it. He avoided looking at James. "Just some silly thing I've been playin' with."

"Sounded pretty good. Who wrote it? You?" James seemed interested, but Frank hesitated to tell him too much.

Frank strolled to the jukebox, dropping a few quarters into it. "I wrote the melody. A friend wrote the lyrics."

"Anyone I know?"

"Nope." *How much longer is he going to ask? Geez, calm down Frank. Take a deep breath and calm down.*

"Okay."

A wave of relief surged through his body. *Whew!* Looking up from the jukebox, he walked over to James and sat down.

"So what's on your mind?" Frank asked, drinking his cola.

"Two things. One—we have our first gig on the Fourth of July in the great state of Arkansas. This means, we'll need to hit the road on the second of July. Second, I'm going to try to call Heather." He sat down next to Frank, wringing his hands over and over again. "It's been awhile and I'd like to see her before we take off. Whaddya think?"

What do I think? You really don't want to know the answer to that. And I don't want to tell you!

Not really knowing exactly what to say or even why James was asking for his permission, Frank shrugged his shoulders. "That's up to you. Just don't be surprised by anything she does. Be persistent. Women have a way of testing a man's sincerity about things like that."

James chuckled in agreement. Frank had a feeling there was some kind of emptiness deep down inside James that was tearing at his heart. He'd been coming to Gabe's every night hoping to see Heather, but she never showed up. Frank knew about the roses he'd sent her and that he didn't care about any other woman.

"Listen, buddy, you're going to have to tell the woman how you feel. I've watched you night after night tearing yourself up. Hell, you don't even look at another woman, and there have been plenty flaunting themselves in front of you." Frank sat at the piano and played the bridge for *You Were Always On My Mind* by Willie Nelson.

"I guess I can't expect her to read my mind." James ran his fingers through his hair, anxiety lining his face. "I'm just gonna have to come out with it."

"Sounds like a plan, man. The sooner the better, if you ask me." Frank stopped playing and pushed away from the instrument. Maybe now things could get back on track before they left town.

Chapter Fifteen

Ring!

Heather stretched, her peaceful sleep disturbed by the phone.

"Kathi, if it's for me, I'm not here. No matter who it is," Heather said as Kathi picked up the receiver.

Kathi nodded. "Hello." Her eyes slanted and filled with suspicion. "No, Heather's not here. Can I take a message?" She grabbed a nearby pen and pad of paper, and scribbled down the message. "Okay, James, I'll tell her you called. Bye."

Kathi placed the receiver in its cradle, shooting Heather a questioning look.

"Don't look at me like that." Heather pulled the blanket closer to her shoulders, shielding herself from her friend.

"Like what?"

"You know…why, what…all those questions I see in your eyes waiting for answers."

"Well, you are going to tell, aren't you?"

"Tell you what? There's nothing to tell except that if he calls again, I'm not here. Okay?" She hoped that discussion would end even though it most likely wouldn't die quietly.

"Heather, what the hell is going on? How can you not even talk to him? He's gorgeous, talented, and is obviously very interested in you. So what gives?"

"You're not going to let it rest, are you?" Heather unwound her body, letting the blanket pool on to her lap.

"Nope."

So much for avoiding that subject.

Heather took a deep breath, winding herself back into a sitting position. "Okay, it's like this. James has what we would call a 'silver spoon' background. His family is everything mine isn't. Well-known, in the public eye, and well-off."

"And your point is what, exactly?"

"The point is I don't want him thinking I'm after his money. We all play around with the fantasy of having someone well-off in our lives, but when it's an arm's length away, it scares the hell out of ya. The way I figure it, if I don't encourage him, maybe he'll go away."

By this time, Heather was pretty confident she'd totally confused Kathi.

"Don't you like him, is that it?"

Yep. If the sound of Kathi's voice indicated anything, she was frustrated, as well.

"The problem is I do like him. Think about it. What do James and I really have in common? Nothing. When I met him, I thought he was just another musician, not the son of one of this town's legendary recording stars."

"It's up to you." Kathi sighed and started up the stairs. She paused long enough to give Heather a hard and determined look. "This guy's not going to give up. I hope you don't sit around waiting too long. Playing hard to get is fine, but all games come to an end sooner or later. There's always a winner…and a loser."

Heather watched Kathi go up the stairs knowing in her heart her friend was right. She couldn't understand why she was so afraid. Why should she be afraid of a man who made her feel comfortable and safe in his arms?

****

James hung up the phone and plopped down in the nearest chair. Frank lounged at the piano, watching him make a fool out of himself. He'd told him he was going to call Heather, even though Frank warned him she might not be home…again. He'd been trying to get ahold of her at work, too, with the answer being the same.

Kathi had told both of them that on at least three occasions, Heather had been home. Frank and Kathi worried about her hiding out so much. All Heather seemed to do was work and then mope around at home. She'd stop coming to Gabe's in fear of seeing James. He prayed she'd snap out of it and return to the real world before he went crazy with worry…and desire.

"Hey, James, how does this sound?" Frank touched the piano keys, singing off tune.

"The melody is fine, but remind me never to ask you to take the mic." Grimacing, he got up from the chair and shuffled over to Frank. "Do you really sing that badly?"

"Must have a frog in my throat," Frank croaked in the middle of a word. "Hey, don't give up on her. She's confused and scared, at least that's what Kathi tells me."

"Why? I'm not going to hurt her." The pain in his heart only intensified, and he wished for a case of whiskey to drown his sorrows in.

"She doesn't trust me, does she?"

"It's not you personally; it's your money and family connections. She wants to make a name for herself, by herself, not through marriage or association. She'll come around." Frank gently touched the piano keys and began the intro to the song he'd been working on.

James picked up his guitar and strummed along with the piano. He'd been hearing it so much, the cords had become second nature to him. In his mind, he understood how Heather felt about making it on her own merit and not on the shirttail of someone else. A woman like her didn't come along very often. Strong, yet vulnerable. Determined, yet unsure.

He wasn't about to give up in any way, shape or form. This lady was worth the struggle, and he'd make sure it came to a pleasurable end. With Heather in his arms, how could it be any other way?

Chapter Sixteen

Heather found herself thinking more and more about James. Kathi had been right; he wasn't giving up. Every day the phone rang, the call would be from James, and the reply was always the same. She wasn't available. No matter how much she avoided him, he wasn't discouraged. A small hidden part of her must have been a little happy about it, because she'd decided to take his next call.

She'd tired of the cat and mouse game. It kept her away from her family and friends. It was self-inflicted, and no one was at fault but herself. Like Kathi had said, all games must come to an end. She'd begun this one; it would only be right she ended it.

Taking a deep breath, she felt a feeling of the weight of world being lifted off her shoulders plunging through her soul. She headed out the door as Kathi pulled up. Before she could turn off her white Sunbird, Heather rapped at her car door window.

"Got any plans when I get off tonight?"

"No, why?"

"Meet me at Gabe's."

Judging by the look on her face, Kathi was in shock. Heather rather enjoyed the startled look in spite of herself.

"Meet me there at 11:00, okay?" Heather climbed behind the wheel of her blue Vega and rolled down her window. "Oh, one more thing. If James calls, tell him I'm at work."

By this time, Kathi was at Heather's window. "This can't go on forever, you know."

"I know. Tell him if he wants to get in touch with me, that's where I'm at."

Kathi let out a little yelp. "You bet!"

Laughing, Heather headed toward work. For the first time in weeks, Heather felt like part of her surroundings. She couldn't remember how, when, or even why the change had taken place, only that it had. She'd been hiding inside herself for so long, she was just now noticing the banners up announcing the upcoming Fourth of July events. She shook her head, wondering how long they'd been there.

****

Heather walked in to Gabe's as if she hadn't stayed away for almost two weeks. Frank sat behind his drums, Brenda ran around from table to table, and Janey handled the bar with her usual ease. Everything was as it should be; her world started to get back on its axis.

Waving to Janey, she grabbed the beer waiting for her and headed out through the patio doors. The night was clear, the air warm, and the stars twinkled like white Christmas lights. She picked a table close enough to see Kathi's car come into the parking lot, but not close enough for anyone to really notice her.

Or so she thought. James sat at a table near her, talking to a group of guys. *Maybe if I sit here quietly, he won't pay me any attention. I'm not ready to face him yet.*

She sat as deep into the night's shadows as she could, afraid if she breathed too loudly he'd hear her. Watching him, she grew more and more anxious by his closeness. Even in the dim outdoor light, his hair shone and his raw features were accented by the play of shadows across his face. She could feel the strength and security of his well-muscled arms around her. He looked and acted like anyone else, not like someone she should fear. So why did she?

Lost in her thoughts, she gasped at the sound of two bottles of beer placed on the table.

"Penny for your thoughts."

Oh God, it's him. Deep breath, just take a deep breath and everything will be okay. She shifted in the chair, trying to ease the surge of desire beginning to run wild.

"Kathi told me you'd be here tonight."

Shadows mixed with a decrease of light can play tricks on a person's mind, but there was no mistaking his sultry voice. A shiver went through her body, leaving goose bumps on her flesh. The figure belonging to the voice she'd come to long for sat down.

"James, how are you?" Her voice trembled even though she tried valiantly to stay calm. *That's it, act like you don't care. He's no one special, no one at all.*

"Makin' a living. You're a hard lady to catch up with. I've called at different times short of the middle of the night." The moonlight caught the concern floating across his face and her heart thumped with glee.

He reached over and took her hand in his. "Let's go inside."

The emotion stirring in his body flowed into her heart. By the look in his eyes, he felt the same as she did. They needed to go inside among people before either of them did something that would embarrass the hell out of one or both of them. There was a time and a place for intimacy, whether it was talking or being physical. The patio of a bar wasn't it.

Slipping back through the patio doors, she saw Kathi sitting at the bar with a smug smile plastered across her face.

"So, friend, how long have you been here?" She sat down in the empty stool next to Kathi.

Kathi took a sip of her beer. "Oh, about five minutes. You all looked busy and I didn't want to intrude."

"I see." The feeling Kathi and Frank had set her up was making her second-guess her decision to come out to Gabe's. Even with James standing behind her, she doubted Kathi's good intentions. Sometimes it's better to stay out of another person's business, no matter what the intention is.

Frank's voice came over the mic as the last chords of *Devil Went Down to Georgia* ended. "I'd like to slow it down a bit and dedicate this next tune to Heather. She's every bit a lady."

The other musicians joined in as Frank sang *Lady*. Heather felt someone take her hand. "Come on, darlin'." James pulled her gently out to the dance floor.

Even if she'd wanted to, she couldn't stop herself from going with him. Her hand instantly went into his as slipped about her waist. Whatever fear she'd thought existed disappeared. The lull of the music and the security of his arms were all she needed to feel lost in the sensual rocking of the dance.

Looking into his eyes, Heather felt the heat of desire burning. Her heart beat in rhythm with his, as if their bodies were joined by that single organ. His breath fluttered through her hair, touching her ear with feather-like softness.

"We need to talk someplace that's quiet and peaceful…away from prying eyes." His whisper caressed her ear, sending a tingling sensation through her body.

"Okay," she said, sweeping the skittering of fear from her mind.

"Will you trust me enough to pick the place?" he asked, nibbling on her ear.

I'm melting like a foolish teenager. Ohhhh, don't stop, please just hold me close. She nodded her head "With one stipulation."

"What's that?" James pulled her closer, if that was even possible.

She took another deep, shaky breath. "You let Frank know where you're taking me."

The band finished with the closing chords and James loosened his hold around her waist. "No problem."

Her gaze followed as he walked over to Frank. The gleaming smile on his face only confirmed her earlier suspicion. She'd been set up. Frank, along with Kathi's help, had made sure James would be there tonight. Smiling to herself, she knew she would have done the same for a friend.

"Everything's set. Are you ready to go?"

Nodding her head, she grabbed her purse and strolled out the door with him. This time, it would be just the two of them. She'd have to rely on her own resources if need be, but she was sure she'd have no need to worry. Not with James holding her hand the way he was.

****

James started the car and headed north. Heather calculated being in the Continental for approximately fifteen minutes before he pulled onto a dirt driveway that ended at the top of a hill.

"Whose house is this?" she asked, peering at the large cabin-like house.

"I shared it at one time with my brother, Utah. But now it's mine." James turned off the ignition and took her hand, sending sparks through her core. "Come on, there's something I want to show you."

Squeezing her hand lightly, James led her through a white gate and around to the front of the house. The view was utterly breathtaking.

A break in the trees revealed the splendor of the warm summer night. The sky was clear and the stars and full moon burned brightly, casting a silvery light on them. From this side of the house, the bright lights of Nashville glowed below.

"It's so beautiful. Almost like you're sitting on top of the world. You'd never guess this was in the city." She listened to the rustling of leaves as a gentle breeze passed through them. The music of the night played around her. Peaceful. Quiet. Serene.

James put his arms around her waist, drawing her closer to him. She gazed into his eyes, feeling the want and desire burning at their surface. She trembled like a leaf and he drew her closer, wrapping her in his arms. His musky smell filled her, awakening every pore.

His hand followed the curve of her back up to her shoulders. Once his hands found her cheeks, he paused only a moment before his mouth found hers. The gentle power devoured her lips. Helpless, she responded to their magic.

She explored his back, running her hands over his muscles and traveling along unknown territory. A wave of desire slammed through her as James gently lowered her to a patch of thick green grass.

Shivers pricked her skin as his mouth left her briefly. He braced their weight as they reached the silky grass. She inhaled deeply as his hands moved slowly up her sides, over the small roundness of her stomach and then lightly brushed across her breasts. His exploration of her ended with hesitation at her chin. Searching his seemingly coal-black eyes, she knew no words needed to be spoken. She was safe. There was nothing there for her to fear.

He sweetly kissed her ear lobes, and she closed her eyes, lost in the freed desires. A small sexual groan escaped when a warm, wet tongue traced her jaw line and then traveled down her chin. Light butterfly kisses followed, sending more shock waves through her.

She arched her back as his strong fingers lightly circled her nipples through her cotton blouse. Running her fingers and hands through James's thick black hair, she found his mouth and claimed it with her own.

As their mouths met, a flash of lightning lit the sky and thunder shook the ground. The rain fell before they could stop kissing.

James pulled her to her feet and they ran for the house. When they had reached the safety of the doorway, their laughter was followed by a long wet kiss, the rain dripping off their bodies.

Unlocking the door, James reached inside and turned on a light. "I'll get you a towel and something dry to put on."

He returned moments later with a big, lush bathrobe and a couple of towels. "There's a bathroom right there. It has everything you need. I'll use the one upstairs." Giving her a quick kiss, he bounded up the stairs. "Just drop your clothes outside the bathroom door. I'll put them in the dryer when I come down."

Heather piled her soaked clothing outside the door, taking her time drying her waterlogged body. She hadn't felt this joyous and alive in so long, she pinched herself, making sure it wasn't a dream.

Wrapping herself in the warm, thick robe, she stepped out of the bath. Her clothes were gone, and somewhere was the hum of a dryer. She rounded the corner and found the fireplace flickering with flames, beckoning her to bask in their warmth.

In the middle of the floor, James sat in a circle of overstuffed pillows. He was draped in a Navajo style robe with a bottle of wine and two glasses next to him. Looking up at her, he held out a hand, inviting her to join him. Sexual warmth spread through her and she snuggled into the warmth of his embrace and the beauty of the fire.

The finished off the wine, and the fire turned to embers as they fell asleep in each other's arms.

****

Frank finished the final touches on "Friends" after what seemed to be months of hard work. He'd listed Heather as the lyricist and himself as the composer. The next step would be the toughest one so far.

He grabbed his suit coat, going over in his head who he was going to see and what he was going to say. He'd decided to play his role as agent to the fullest. Shadow Records was top of the list today. The day before, he'd spent a couple of hours each with Golden Era Plantation, CBS Songs, and EPIC Records.

The meetings had been okay. CBS Songs seemed to be the most interested of the three, although each said they'd get back to him in a few days. He didn't want to use his position at Shadow to get the song noticed, but after a good night's sleep, he decided he'd have nothing to lose. Would they say no to the man who'd given them Utah Sheridan and Emerald Braun on a silver platter?

He hoped not.

Frank adjusted his tie, picked up the portfolio containing the sheet music, and walked out the door. Plopping down in the driver's seat, he fired up the van and made his way downtown to the heart of the city.

His nerves were popping, and having to deal with the morning traffic and tourists didn't help any. He'd put a lot of hard work and many hours into making sure the melody was just right, hoping someone would see the feeling and potential of this song.

Frank parked his vehicle in the first available spot near the Shadow Records building. With portfolio in hand, he took a long deep breath to calm his nerves. Shadow had become one of the biggest recording companies around; scoring with them would be amazing.

Once inside, the cool air conditioning chased the heat from his body. He made his way to the elevators, feeling a bit more at ease.

The meeting lasted about forty-five minutes. Frank performed the tune and gave his sales pitch. They liked it, and wanted to see if they could find a fit with one of their artists. They'd keep him in mind, thank you.

He'd give them until he got back from Arkansas before contacting them again. Nothing to do now but wait.

Chapter Seventeen

Several weeks later

Heather had a hard time believing she'd woken up that morning in James's arms. The fire had gone out long before then, but his massive strong arms were wrapped around her.

Even now, the silky bath water warmed her and she could still hear the evenness of his breathing and smell the faint scent of musk. She'd felt totally safe and secure.

It had been over breakfast when James reminded her he'd be leaving for a few days to a traditional Fourth of July celebration in Arkansas that he didn't dare cancel. That seemed centuries away, when it had only been a few days.

She stepped out of the cooling water, drying her body with a large bath sheet. As she got ready for bed, her mind kept telling her he'd be back soon. She turned the light down to a low beam, opened the blinds enough to see the clear summer night, and curled up in an easy chair. She gazed out into the night, silently praying for his safe and quick return home.

A smile came to her face as she looked out into the star-filled night. It reminded her of that night at James's home the very same night she'd come to realize her feelings for him.

Without giving it a second thought, she picked up her notebook and pencil. The lead flowed across the page, leaving the night's feelings behind.

I remember the first time we met
Your eyes full of warmth and your smile so inviting I thought I was lost in time
I was shy at first and unsure ...
But you showed me it was gonna be fine
You took me in your arms and we took a walk in the starry moonlit night
Our passion so fresh and new...
It was as if time stood still
A few days have gone by now...

I'm sippin' on some rosé wine and wonderin'
Will we soon return to that time and place
Where we had only each other on our minds
Lost in a dream-like world
Not knowin' time or space
Just our newfound love

Heather read her words once the pencil came to rest. Emotion rushed over her, filling her heart. Closing the notebook, she turned out the lights then slipped between her bed sheets, falling into a peaceful sleep.

****

At three o'clock Sunday morning, the bus pulled into James's driveway. They'd loaded up the bus and left Arkansas as soon as their last tune was done. With everyone totally exhausted, they were all glad to finally be home.

James offered up his home for those too tired to make the drive to their own beds. As usual, everyone accepted the invitation. Unloading a suitcase each, the five-piece band made their phone calls to their wives or girlfriends.

After getting everyone settled in, James picked up the phone himself. He would have talked to Heather when Frank had called Kathi, but since Kathi was house-sitting for Frank, it was impossible. Pushing the numbers that would allow him to hear Heather's soft southern accented Yankee voice, he listened to the ringing on the other end.

"Hello," a sleepy female voice answered.

"Hi, Darlin'. I'm home."

Chapter Eighteen

Heather could hardly contain herself. James would arrive in less than forty-five minutes, and she wasn't anywhere near ready to see him. She'd been floating on a cloud ever since he called to let her know he was back.

She pinned her hair up on the sides, allowing her feathery bangs to fall freely. All she needed was a red checkered dress, and she'd look as country as country could get...old country, that is. The thought of an old Ma Kettle movie caused a giggle to surface as she went downstairs into the kitchen.

She pulled the roast beef from the oven and stuck a fork into the carrots and potatoes.

Bzzzzzz!

Damn! Twenty minutes early. She walked into the living room, pausing at the wall mirror long enough to put an unruly wisp of hair back in place. Her palms sweaty, she pulled open the door holding the breath she'd just inhaled.

"Hi, Heather."

"Frank." She playfully punched her closest friend's future husband in the arm, overwhelmed by disappointment, relief, and frustration.

"Hey, what's that for?" Frank asked, rubbing his arm as he walked into the living room. "Damn, have you been hitting the punching bag lately? That smarts."

"I thought you were James." She followed him into the duplex, willing her jumbled insides to settle down. "Why are you here anyway?"

"Ah, Kathi. I'm here to pick her up."

"Oh, yeah." She ran the palms of her hands over her skirt. "I forgot."

"Forgot!" Kathi's voice boomed down the stairs. A smile as wide as the Mississippi on her face, she stood at the bottom, hands on her hips. "Come on, Frank, let's go where people remember who we are." Flashing Heather a quick wink, Kathi took hold of Frank's elbow and led him toward the front door.

"Okay." Frank gave Heather a brotherly smile. "See ya later, Yank."

Heather closed the door, thinking how only a few months ago, everyone's focus had been on her and Frank; now it was on James and their relationship. It amazed her how quickly things change. Heather shook her head, turning her attention to the dining room table. She wanted to make sure everything was perfect, from the candles right down to the spotless silverware.

Bzzzzzz!

"Now what the…?" she said, pulling open the door. "James!"

Nothing about him had changed. She hadn't thought it would. Heather stood back, unsure of knowing whether to throw her arms around him and shower him with kisses or not. She didn't have to worry. James pressed his body against hers. His hungry kisses told her he'd missed her as much as she did him.

"Damn, it's good to hold you again," he said, breaking the kiss.

"I missed you, too," she replied, soaking up the warmth and need in his eyes. "More than I ever thought I would."

"Heather." James barely got her name out before they were kissing each other again. "Hey, what's that smell?"

"Oh, no!" Heather pulled out of James' arms, racing for the kitchen. She yanked the nearly ruined dinner from the oven when he pulled up behind her.

"Any damage?" James asked, drawing her to his chest after the pan barely made it to the counter.

"No, but there will if we keep this up." She swatted him with a potholder and shooed him from the kitchen. "It'll be ready in a sec. Now get out of here."

****

James ducked away, barely feeling the potholder smack his ass. Walking back into the living room, he looked around. He'd never been in Heather's house, and he wanted to learn more about her.

The room definitely held a woman's touch, nothing close to the masculinity of his home. There were Victorian-style pictures with soft, muted colors on the walls. Crocheted dollies under the pitcher and bowl sets on various tables. And the sounds of a woman in the kitchen along with the smell of a home-cooked meal.

James liked this female touch. He liked it very much.

The wait had been worth it after all. Heather could fill that void in his life. Closing his eyes, James pictured what it would be like to have Heather in his home, standing over the stove with a toddler tugging on her apron. Old fashioned was definitely what he wanted. Just a touch of old fashioned, in harmony with a modern kind of woman.

A woman like Heather.

"Table's ready, James. Let's eat."

Heather stood over the table, leaning slightly to light the dinner candles. With the lights off, she was a vision waiting for him to come to dinner.

"Come on, before it gets cold," she purred, reaching for a bottle of wine.

James came to the table and began carving the roast. He watched her pour the bubbly drink into their glasses and a vision of him carving a Thanksgiving Day turkey popped into his head. He could almost smell the cranberries, sweet potatoes, and gravy.

"How's that?" he asked, feeling quite proud of his work

"Great. Do you think we really should eat such a work of art though?" She laughed, sitting across from him.

"Well…it would be a shame to waste it."

"You're right. Let's just eat it and forget about being pretty."

Much to Heather's delight, the meal turned out perfectly. The wine chilled to the right temperature, and the candles hadn't dripped on her Grandmother's special tablecloth. James ate two helpings of everything, looking like a full and satisfied cat.

They'd talked about anything and everything—the gig, Frank and Kathi, each other's families, Heather's job, anything that would allow them to learn more about each other.

"Whew, I'm stuffed," James groaned as he got up, leaning over to give her a kiss. "Thanks. It was good. I didn't know you could cook like this."

"There's a lot of things about me you don't know." She continued clearing the table.

"Given the chance, I'd like to learn," James said, making his way between the sofa and coffee table. "What's this?"

He picked up a binder lying under the table, "Pictures?"

Shit, I forgot about those. It took her only three steps before she reached out for it. "Nothing."

James yanked it out of her grasp, spilling loose papers onto the carpet. "Sorry." picking up a sheet, he read the words. He gathered the rest of the sheets, and his eyes swept across each one.

This was a part of her life she wasn't ready for him to see. She'd written about her love for him on each of those pages, exposing her to him as if she were naked to the world.

"Did you write these?" James turned the pages over and over, studying each one.

Embarrassed and a bit irritated, she snatched the binder and its contents out of his hands. She hugged the precious pages to her chest, turning away from James. A weak "Yes" was all she could muster.

"Why are you hiding them?" James embraced her from behind, giving her a sense of security. "From what I saw, they looked good. Let me read them, Heather, please."

She turned and gazed into his eyes, seeing the truth there. Forcing herself to trust him, she passed the binder to him. She couldn't believe how careless she'd been in leaving it out and then handing them over to him so easily. No one, not even Frank or Kathi, to her knowledge, had seen what was in the binder. When she was ready, Heather had wanted to pick and choose the ones for others to see.

What did it matter now? Her only consolation was she knew James wouldn't laugh at her or her feelings.

****

Feelings…that's what they'd first had in common. An experience of feelings and need. Heather with Josh; James with Suzette. They'd both confided in each other about their broken hearts; it was a way of letting each other know they needed to take it slow. How much of this was about Josh? He wasn't sure he could stand the pain in her words.

Taking the papers from Heather, James walked back over to the sofa and sat, reading first one page and then another. Finishing each page, he saw the woman he knew existed, a woman who was loving, caring, and sensitive. A woman he found himself falling deeply and truly in love with.

He especially liked *Whispering Wind*. "These are good, Heather. What do you plan to do with them?"

She stood several feet from him, wringing her hands in worry. "I'd like to maybe…well someday…you're gonna think this is silly, but…get them published." Her face flushed with embarrassment. How could she feel embarrassed over words as wonderful as the ones he'd just experienced?

He rose and took a cautious step toward the woman who moved his heart in more ways than one.

"A songwriter. You want to be a songwriter? That's great." He took her trembling hands in his own, hoping to reassure her. "There's a couple I'd like to work with you on, if that's okay."

"I don't know." She looked into his eyes. "I'll think about it, okay?"

"Okay." Seeing the uncertainty pool in her eyes, he pulled her close to him. Her heart raced against his chest, spreading warmth and desire through him. "It's warm tonight. Let's take a walk."

Nodding her head, they walked out the door into the star-filled night holding each other's hand. James knew in that moment he'd never let go of her.

Chapter Nineteen

Taking in the floral scents of the night, Heather felt relief as she slid her hand easily into James's. The anxiety over the song book vanished as if the incident hadn't occurred.

Dusk made its mark on the world as they walked toward a small, isolated park near Heather's house. They'd be able to feed the geese and enjoy the quiet serene surroundings, something she felt they desperately needed.

As they walked along in silence, Heather sorted out her jumbled mind. So many feelings to deal with. She was in love with James, no doubt about it. The accidental finding of her songs unnerved her, but not enough to make her pull away from him. James's suggestion he'd work on a couple with her made her feel safe in placing them in his hands.

She had a few songs that were more than just okay. It was why she'd decided to stay in Nashville...to become a noted songwriter. The man she loved felt they were good enough to record, and it scared the hell out of her.

It scared her through her bones, leaving nothing but pieces of shattered marrow.

She'd have to come to terms with it before James started helping her. She didn't want to take advantage of his friendship and love, which was what worried her most. Would he eventually come to think that of her? To think she wasn't any different from the other women he met daily?

I love him for his heart, not his accounts.

****

James thought about dinner, Heather, and her songs. He'd been right in taking Frank's advice. This lady was indeed a rare breed of woman; his love and want for her grew deeper. He'd realized how deep those feelings were while in Arkansas. Each song he'd sung was for her. Each thought held a place for her.

Putting his arm around her shoulder, he pulled her closer as they strolled under the streetlamps. For the first time in years, Suzette's memory no longer hurt. No ugly shadows, only reality and Heather.

At the park, he chose a table canopied under two trees. The night was perfect…warm and peaceful. The type of night two people in love wait for, yearn for.

Sitting down, he pulled her to his lap. She was fast becoming his love of a lifetime, he knew it deep in his heart.

The silence of the night felt as natural to him as opening up about his past and the love he once thought he had.

"Heather," he started, inhaling the lavender scent of her soft hair. "I need to know if this is real…that you feel as I feel."

She snuggled closer in his arms, kissing his neck. "I can't see my life without you, James."

"I need to know in what capacity, to be assured that you'll not fly away once you get your wings. I couldn't take it if you turned out to be like Suzette."

A moment of silence passed between them.

James got up from the table, leaving the warmth and security of Heather's body. He walked to the water's edge, thinking about her, until he felt arms slip gently around his waist. Her head rested against his back as she hugged him close.

Gazing into the moonlight reflecting on the water, he turned to take her in his arms. Seeing the love, friendship, and understanding in her seawater-hazel eyes, his hands drew her face to meet his.

Heather caught a glimpse of the tear trickling down James's cheek. The warmth of his lips made her body melt into his, entwined. The kiss turned from a soft gentle caress to one of starved passion feeding upon their love.

Their heated desires drove their tongues in a wild dance. The pressure of his body guided her down to the grass. Her will to resist flew away with the geese as their bodies came together in the grass.

In one swift movement, the sounds of the night surrounded them. Fiery passion burned faster and hotter. The weight of him and the aroma of his musky skin enhanced her desire for him. She shifted her hips, bringing him closer to her.

James's hand moved up her inner thigh, her stockings the only barrier between their skin. The sensual touch found its way to her garter-covered soft, furry mound. A sensual moan escaped into the night. She pushed against his hand, increasing the pleasure mounting between her thighs.

His long, strong fingers slid under her panties. She shuddered at his touch. His fingers entwined with her downiness, the moistness of her desire for him growing.

James repositioned so he could gaze into the face of the woman who'd stolen his heart the moment he'd seen her. His hand moved up the curve of her waist and onto her breasts. His breathing increased and he hungrily devoured the sweetness of her lips and tongue.

Her nipples grew taut when the softness of his tongue played with hers. The straps of her dress slipped down, exposing her taut, pulsing nipples.

He covered every inch of her heaving breasts with kisses. Material slid exposing the rest of her to him. He ached to be inside her.

Heather moved her hand along James's back, losing all sense of her surroundings. There was only James and herself. Her only reality was the feel and smell of the man she so deeply loved.

She opened her eyes to see James lying naked next to her. The night's starlight shone faintly on his muscular shape. Slowly and gently, he pressed his body onto hers.

Their hearts beat like drums, hands caressed flesh, lips tasted salty, warm skin as bodies met and shuddered.

When the skyrocketing came down from the stars, they quickly dressed and hurried arm in arm through the night.

Chapter Twenty

Frank worked hard on the song he'd pitched all over town. Night after night, he arrived at rehearsal for The Night Ramblers a few hours earlier to go over the current version. Sometimes it would be a note change, while other times it would involve entire stanzas being replaced. Every time he'd change it, the playback would be to himself or Kathi later that same evening.

Tonight was no exception. An hour before the schedule rehearsal, Frank arrived at James's to work on the melody. The sound of a guitar strumming a different tune snapped him out of his deep concentration. He'd been so engrossed, he didn't notice the rest of the band silently listening and watching.

"Hey, Frank," James sang, continuing to play along, "can we get on with rehearsal?"

"Huh? Oh yeah, sure." Frank sat up, gawking at the rest of the guys shaking their heads. *How in the hell did they manage to get in here so quietly? His truck can sound like a Harley most nights.*

"All right then, let's do it," James said, motioning for the rest of the band.

Running through their usual lineup and halfway through *Snowy Firelight*, James stopped abruptly.

"Y'all know this set up so well you could sing and play it in your sleep. Let's try something new." Looking straight into Frank's eyes, James walked across the room. "Frank here's been workin' on a new tune for a few months. Maybe we can help him out."

Frank's heart hit the floor hard and fast. A trio of voices agreed, and Frank stammered as he quickly tried to put his thoughts together. "Ah, okay." Maybe this was just the break he needed. Some other input wouldn't hurt.

"It's in the key of D, and the melody goes something like this."

Stroking the keys, Frank coaxed the piano into releasing the flow of music from beginning to end. "James, you know this pretty well and it's in your range. Here's the lyrics."

Handing the sheet music over to James, Frank didn't wait for him to look it over. He returned to his drums, gave the signal, and the piano began a short intro before the rest of the band joined in. Following along on his guitar, James sang the lyrics with perfect timing. Halfway through, he stopped, staring at the paper in utter surprise.

Each of the band members followed suit, waiting to find out what James had to say.

"James, you okay, buddy?" Frank rested his hand on the shoulder of an unusually silent man.

"Frank, I'd like to talk to you about this, in private." Questions filtered from his eyes, changing to worry in his words. "Take an hour break, guys."

When the wondering whispers finally faded away, Frank remained at his drums, head in his hands. James was reading the lyrics for the third time since dismissing the other band members.

"I don't believe it." James put down his guitar, then walked over to Frank. "Heather wrote this, didn't she?"

"James…:

"I know she did. I saw all her songs the other night and this is one of them. How did you get it?" Menace edged his words, Frank felt he was walking on thin ice.

Frank sat back on his stool, running his hand over his face. "It was a gift."

"A gift? For what?" James didn't move. If looks could kill, Frank would have died before he took his next breath.

"Yeah. Remember that night of the…" Frank explained the night he tried to kiss Heather. He ran through the story, unfolding it all for James.

"You were in love with her?" James asked, jealous disbelief echoing in his question.

"Yeah, and I still love her, but as a very good friend. Nothing more, James." *I should have come clean on this when I fell for Kathi. I should have known it would eventually catch up to me.*

James swung around, setting his guitar onto its stand. "All this work on a song, for what?"

"Not for what, for who. Heather. I've been trying to get someone to really listen to it, but with no luck." Frank told him about the hours he'd spent down on Music Row pitching the tune to anyone who would listen. "Shadow is considering it. So far, just polite thanks but no thanks."

"Why didn't you come to me?" James asked, his back still to Frank.

It made him nervous; a man as big as James could give a little guy like him a lot of pain.

"Listen, James, Heather doesn't know about this. I didn't want to take advantage of our friendship and business relationship. She has talent—raw talent, but talent nonetheless."

"Okay, I get the picture." Staring aimlessly at the paper, deep thought replaced the bewilderment on James' face. "Frank, I want to help. We can make this a business deal. You know we need new material. And if we all work hard, we could have this ready before the next road trip." His voice held nothing but sincerity.

"In two weeks? Are you nuts?" The offer was good, he just wasn't sure about the timing.

"Nope. The credit will go to you and Heather. If it works, maybe we'll go national with it as an album cut or even a single." By the look on James's face, Frank knew better than to second guess him anymore. All in all, he couldn't chase away the nagging feeling it was all too quick to be done right.

"I don't know. I just…"

"Let's run through it once with the rest of the guys and see how they feel. If they like it, we'll do it. Okay?"

Now that seems a bit more reasonable. If James is leading with his heart instead of his head, the rest of the band will prove that.

"Okay," Frank agreed, hoping he was doing the right thing. In reality, no fault no harm…he had nothing to lose and possibly a hell of a lot to gain.

James walked out into the front room and called the guys together. Going over the plan, they ran through each instrument's section of the melody. Once they all understood, Frank gave a four count with his sticks, then listened as the piano intro began the opening chords. He picked up the beat along with the steel and base guitars. James joined in with lyrics and lead licks.

The tune quietly ended followed by a moment of silence.

"All right!" They all screamed out in unison agreement.

Looked to Frank like *Friends* was their next project.

"Well, Frank?" James said, half asking and half laughing.

"Okay, it's a deal." Frank laughed, nodding his head in defeat. "But, before we take it out on the road, I'd like to debut it at Gabe's and get Heather's approval also."

"Deal."

Frank shook James' hand, sealing the deal. Rehearsal of the new song put a much-needed spark back into the band. Each set rang out, growing closer and closer to perfection.

Chapter Twenty-One

The Night Ramblers worked hard and furious getting the new song ready. Frank and James continuously disagreed, until things finally came together. Frank didn't know who was more relieved...him or James.

Not wanting to waste any time, Frank arranged with Kathi to make sure Heather showed up at Gabe's. The question was whether she would get there without giving Kathi a hard time about it. He really wanted her to be surprised at the entire deal—what he'd done with her poem, James wanting to record the song version of it. So much depended upon Heather approving what they'd done.

Arriving around eight, Frank had a couple of beers and waited for the rest of the band to show up. He went over the plan in his head. Heather and Kathi would come in around ten, with James arriving shortly before then. They'd be able to go over everything one last time, making sure it went as planned.

Where in the hell are they? Heather'll be here in less than thirty minutes, damn it. Frank was drumming out the closing to *Mountain Music* when James and the rest of the band walked in. Lee must have noticed at the same time, because he was calling for a break like Frank had discussed with him before taking the stage.

Frank left the wall of drums and sauntered up to the bar. "Okay, James," he said, placing his hands on the rail in front of him, "how are we going to do the rest of this?"

"I have no idea," James said, looking him in the eye. "I couldn't come up with anything solid. I guess the band'll take the stage, open up with a Jennings tune, and then go into *Friends*. The only thing I can say is to follow my lead."

Frank took a long swig from the beer in front of him. "Follow your lead? Are you sure this is going to work?"

"No. Here come Heather and Kathi now," James said, quickly turning away from the door.

Frank watched Kathi and Heather walk over to their end of the bar. The wink Kathi sent signaled everything was okay. Heather slid up behind James, wrapping her arms around him and kissing his neck.

"Hi, Hon, what are you doing here?" she asked, smiling over at Frank as James turned around.

"Frank came up with the idea of trying out some new stuff before the road trip and I agreed," he said, smacking her squarely on the lips for everyone to see…including Frank.

"Really? So you've got talent plus brains. Nice idea, Frank."

"Thanks," Frank said, raising his beer to her. *So far, so good.*

Heather smiled and then reached out to give Frank a pat on the shoulder.

"So what was the pow-wow all about?" Kathi asked. "It looked like some important business goin' on."

Frank put his arm around her waist, pulling his bride-to-be closer to him. He loved the way she felt in his arms, as if she belonged there. "See how you are. Not even married yet, and you're already askin' questions," he lightly teased, then placed a soft kiss on her lips.

"Just practicing. You know what they say…practice makes perfect," Kathi teased.

"And no secrets!"

"No secrets," Kathi laughed, after she punched him in the arm.

"Ouch!"

"Hen-pecked already," James joked, shaking his head. "I'll have no home life adversely affecting any of our professional business."

"You wait. Your day's comin', maybe sooner than you think," Frank quipped, then vacated the bar stool and headed back to the sanctuary of his drums.

Better get this show on the road.

He leaned in to the mic. "We have a fellow musician in the crowd, which is nothing unusual, of course, who'd like to perform a bit for y'all. And I believe the man brought his own band with him, too."

Now or never, Frank.

"James, it's your spotlight."

****

Heather wondered why Kathi had insisted on her going out to Gabe's after work. She knew James and Frank were heading out on the road in a few days, and the last thing she wanted was hanging out with everyone when she could be snuggled at home with her man.

She watched James and the other band members make themselves comfortable behind borrowed equipment. James picked up Lee's guitar, pulling the strap over his head and around his shoulder with his gazed locked on her.

"You know what they say. Good help is hard to find these days, Frank." James kept his attention on Heather while the rest of the band adjusted the instruments. "For those of you who don't know who I am, I'm James Sheridan and the boys behind me are The Night Ramblers. We're gonna do a couple of tunes for y'all. One by Waylon that I'm sure ya'll will recognize and then another one that's brand new for us. So have a good time and dance if you feel the need to move your feet."

Frank gave a four count with his drumsticks and the band broke into *Are You Sure Hank Done It This Way* by Waylon Jennings. Frank sang the lead vocals, bringing back memories of her first few times in Gabe's. It was one of her fondest memories and one of her favorite songs.

Heather glanced around. A lot of people from backstage of the Opry were there. What surprised her more was James's father walking through the door. Rona and Robert trailed right behind him.

"Hi, Darlin'," Will Sheridan said, giving her a fatherly kiss on the cheek. Will's presence in the small club drew a number of stares; the man just didn't go out in public that often unless it was to perform. He turned to Robert, a long arm and large hand extended out, and took her cousin's hand in acknowledgement.

"What brings you out, Will?" Heather hoped the confusion racing through her mind hadn't settled onto her words. She was curious at his presence.

"James called saying he needed my opinion on a new song," Will answered, waving off a beer from the bartender.

A stream of relief crashed through her confusion. It seemed very reasonable that James would ask his father for his opinion. Not likely, but reasonable.

Applause drew Heather's attention back to the stage and the man she loved. Her heart spun as he pulled the guitar to one side and reached for the microphone.

"Thank you very much," he said, bowing slightly. "As I said before, we have a new tune for y'all." His gaze drifted over the crowd until it locked in with Heather's. An electrical, sensual need shot through her. She quivered with anticipation. "It was written by a dear, close friend of ours for an equally close friend. It's a song about love and friendship. Heather, honey, this is for you and all the beauty inside you."

She returned his look of love as the piano started the opening chords, followed by the drums and guitars. A hush fell over the bar with the softness of the melody. James's sang the words Heather had written for Frank.

Mixed feelings rushed through her. Blinking away the water invading her eyes, she couldn't believe those were her words put to music. But they were and they fit perfectly, reflecting the emotions she'd felt Frank once had for her.

James finished the last of the lyrics. The guitars faded out and the drums fell silent, allowing the piano to finish the song as it had begun it…alone. The last note softly escaped the chords. Silence hung in the air for only a second, followed by hooting, whistling and clapping from the crowd. Obviously they loved it. They loved her song…*MY song!*

****

James felt a strong hand grab his. Meeting the same dark eyes as his own, his father put his arms around him showing a rare public display of emotion. Thanking his father, he spotted Heather making her way to the stage. The expression on her face revealed nothing, but he knew her well enough to know she'd expect answers from him.

Heather stayed close to him as he fielded questions about the writer and accepted congratulations. He put his arm around her, drawing her close to him. He wanted to be sure she felt included in the excitement. After all, it had been her words they shared with the crowd tonight.

"Listen, everybody. Listen!" He yelled, getting the attention of the people milling around him. "All your questions will be answered in time. Some important details have to be worked out before anything else can be done or said."

Half whispering and half yelling, he put his lips close to Heather's ear. He inhaled the lavender scent that was her and her alone. "Let's get out of here. We've got to talk, okay?"

He gathered her closer to him as he pushed their way out of Gabe's and into the muggy August night.

****

"Heather." James held her hand, wetting his lips and looking past her shoulder into the darkened trees behind them. "I want to explain and tell you what we have on our minds."

She waited for him to tell her about their plan. She'd hear him out, even though she was full of questions. She was both scared and excited about the prospect of her song being more than words written on a piece of paper.

"Yes, the song is the one you wrote for Frank. He's been working on it for several months. I played the melody with him so many times. He kept the lyrics a well-guarded secret." His hand felt clammy against hers. She was glad when he released it and wiped his palms along his pant leg. "Anyway, at rehearsal last week, I suggested that we take a look at it and help him out. It took a bit of convincing, but he finally relinquished it over to the band. It wasn't until he handed me the sheet music and I began to sing. I knew they were your words."

She held back the tears threatening to flood her eyes. She could see how important it was for him to tell her this. She longed to throw her arms around him, tell him it was okay.

"Heather, honey, I love you. You know I'd never do anything to hurt you, don't you?" he asked, worry slicing its way into his eyes.

"Of course," she whispered, no longer able to fight the tears spilling down her cheeks.

"This song is good. The people loved it." James gingerly pushed away the salty tears. "I want to take it on the road. Maybe put it on an album."

"James, I don't know. Why didn't you let me in on this? Why hide it?" Her voice shook slightly. She wasn't mad at him...or Frank, for that matter. She just wanted to know why they'd kept it secret.

"It was to be a surprise. No one but Frank and I know you wrote it. If you don't want us to do it, we won't."

No matter how much she felt left out in the dark, the strong man who had her heart looked on the verge of defeat. She couldn't do that to him. Scared of what it could mean to her, she sighed deeply. Together, they'd make it work.

"Okay, but can we work out the details later?"

"Yes," James answered, capturing her mouth with his lips. The salty tears resting in the corners of her mouth disappeared with each kiss.

"James, there you two are!"

Parting, they looked toward the voice and the figure belonging to James's father.

"Come on back inside. Your presence is needed on stage again."

"Why?" they asked, their voices in perfect harmony.

"Don't know except Frank wants ya." With that, Will turned and then walked back through the patio doors and into the crowded bar.

James turned toward Heather, his arms holding her close to him. "Ready?" he whispered softly through her hair.

"As ready as I'll ever be," she said, wondering where the strength in those words came from. She was trembling inside like a girl on her first prom date.

"Can we let some of it out of the bag?" he asked, his eyes filled with pride.

Heather drew herself up straight, threw back her shoulders, and then took his hand. "Let's do it, only don't leave me alone."

She was scared of everyone inside, scared of what this song composed out of friendship could mean—so scared, she squeezed his hand tighter and tighter, her nails digging into his palm.

Chapter Twenty-Two

In the soundproofed walls of James's basement, Heather vividly remembered what took place just days before. He'd kept his promise. He'd only said the song would most likely be on the next album, that he was taking it on the road that weekend for the first time to test it out.

She was grateful he didn't reveal her as the songwriter. As much as she loved and wanted the recognition, she wasn't quite ready for it. Now all that had to change, if the road trip had been a success.

They were all gathered to discuss the road trip and the success or failure of the tune. Looking over his notes, James sat on the arm of her chair.

"Well, this is going to be short for some and long for others." He shuffled the papers he held and then looked around at the men who'd dedicated their lives to him and his music for years.

"The gig was great. Essentially, I have no qualms about anything or anyone. The new song worked out fine. Heather, that's why I asked you to join us." His hand rested lightly on her shoulder, sending a blast of warmth through her body reminding her how much she'd missed him. "Other than that, and if no one has anything to add, you can all go except for Frank."

"When's the next gig?"

"Not for a while. The next one's scheduled in October during the DJ convention. After that, it'll be slow for road trips, so we'll be home more often." James stood, taking the warmth of his body with him. "If there's nothing else, let's wrap it up for tonight."

James walked the rest of the band out, leaving her to drill Frank about the song.

"It went over well?" she asked, nervously waiting for his hopefully truthful answer.

"Very well. In fact, maybe even more so than *Snowy Firelight*," he said, his smile broader than the Cheshire cat's.

She sat back in the chair, her heart pounding with astonishment. "Are you serious?"

"Yeah." Frank's voice held a serious note to it, bringing her down from the safety of the cloud she'd climbed onto. "I know what I did with your words was sneaky, but damn it, girl! You obviously want and desire it, but where the hell is your drive? It feels to me like you've lost the desire I saw in you when you first came to town. It's like you gave up before even starting," Frank said, getting up from his place on the sofa. "Thank God James volunteered to help me. He honestly believes it'll work, Heather. You have to make a decision tonight."

How could Frank for one minute even think she didn't want this? That she didn't want her dream to come true? What had she done to make him think that? The muffled sound of James' footsteps rushed through Heather.

"Has Frank filled you in?" James asked, stretching out in a chair. His fingers interlocked behind his head, the only thing between the wall and his wavy dark hair. She itched to run her fingers through the strands.

"Filled me in? Sort of. I guess the song was a success." She mulled over the implication of what Frank had said moments before. "And that everything depends on me, but hasn't told me how or why."

"*That's* an understatement," James said, resting his hands on either side of those long legs of his.

She caught a quick wink between him and Frank. *These two are up to no good, again!*

"I want to put it on the next album; cut it as a single," James said, his voice clearly full of business and nothing more.

"You want what?" she asked, not believing the tone of the words. It was more of a statement, a demand from a man used to getting his own way. This was a side of him Heather hadn't seen before and frankly, wasn't sure she wanted any part of.

"I want to record it," James said using the demanding tone. Obviously, he wasn't used to dealing with someone who might actually say "No" to him. *Damn it, he knows better than to use that one with me!*

"My song. You want to record MY song? And in that tone of voice? Damn it, James! You act like it's your song," she cried out, trying to curb the anger and frustration building inside her.

"Not really," he said, walking toward her, his body rigid. She figured he was trying to maintain control of a temper she didn't know existed. But then again, she'd never seen him in business mode before. "It would belong to all three of us. You, my dear, get credit for the lyrics. Frank, the melody. And me as the singer as it climbs the charts."

Heather wiggled in the chair, uneasy and unnerved by his self-centeredness and cockiness. *I hate this business already, and I'm just starting.*

"May I say something?" Frank interjected, pacing the floor. "All we can do is try it. James, you could have your attorney draw up the necessary legal documents. Heather, I know how much you trust Robert. Why not have him look over the documents before you sign? As for me, I'm all for the idea." Braced against a wall, Frank looked at them both with an expected look on his face.

Why hadn't she thought of that? Knowing Robert would have her back and best interests in mind eased her doubts considerably. She loved and trusted James, but when it came to business ventures, blood was thicker than water at this point.

"Okay, Frank." She prayed her words carried the air of confidence lacking in her heart at the moment. "We can't split this three ways 'cause the guys deserve something, too. How about if each of the other members gets ten percent, which would leave us sixty between us. For this one tune, we would get twenty each."

"You're right about the rest of the band, Heather. It wouldn't hurt if they got a little bigger piece of the pie," Frank said, slapping his hands together. "I don't have a problem with it."

"James?" she asked, wondering if he'd go along with them. It was, after all, two against one, him being the one.

James walked around the room, running his hands through his hair. A slick smile tilted his mouth, and he turned to her. "Under one condition. No, let me make that TWO conditions."

She shook her head. *Now what did he come up with? Glad to know he's resourceful, but gosh, there's a limit...isn't there?*

"Okay." She sighed. "What are they?"

"Heather, no matter what you write from this point forward, I get first crack at it," James insisted, his face glowing with pride before turning to Frank. "And Frank, that you and only you write the melody for those songs. Those are my conditions, take 'em or leave 'em."

A rush of tears filled Heather's eyes. "That's it? I'd be nuts not to take those conditions," she said, wrapping her arms around her love.

"You helped me out with it, buddy," Frank said from his position against the wall.

"You did ninety percent of it Frank. All I did was hone in on what you'd already done, right?" James asked, pulling her closer to him.

God, how she loved the feel of his arms around her. How could she, for even a second, doubt his reasons for wanting to record her song? Being scared had overridden her love and trust in him, it would never happen again.

"Yeah, but..."

"But nothin'. That's the condition. Decide, Frank," James finalized, his voice indicating he had no intention of changing the conditions.

"Shit, James, you drive a hard bargain," Frank stammered, looking at

Heather as if asking what he should do. No way in hell was she going to tell him how to make up his mind. He was a big boy and very capable of doing it himself. "Hell, why not."

The tears she'd been holding back seeped from her eyes. She'd surrounded herself with good people, and wouldn't change it even for the million-dollar jackpot.

James broke away from her and stepped over to the bar at the other end of the room. He pulled out an ice bucket containing a bottle of champagne, followed by three glasses. They toasted and then discussed James going to his attorney and Heather having Robert look over the documents before she signed them.

She had Frank to thank for actually giving her a push down her dream path. He'd been right—she had lost track of her goals when James came into her life. It had happened so fast. It seemed like yesterday she'd stepped off that Greyhound bus.

Snuggling down into the corner of the sofa, she drifted off to sleep. She didn't move until she felt James carry her to his bedroom. He gently laid her on the bed and opened the patio door blinds to the starry night.

He smiled at her, sending hot shivers over her body. *Good-looking, great performer, business-wise and a romantic…what more could a girl ask for?*

Evidently, he had the answer for that. He stripped out of his jeans and t-shirt, leaving them in a heap at his feet. He slowly undressed her of every stitch of her clothing before gathering her in his arms. Skin touching skin, she was safe. Safe from the sharks in the music business. Safe from her fears of swimming in their waters.

The steadiness of their breathing, combined with the sound of the night seeping through the slightly opened balcony doors, lulled her into a restful and satisfied sleep.

Chapter Twenty-Three

Heather sat on a stool behind the record studio's engineers. Over the past month or so, James had been spending most of his time here working the upcoming album to perfection. *I still can't believe it.*

With the amount of equipment it took to get the music recorded and re-recorded to perfection, she was surprised anything was ever finished. Thankfully, even though the album was going slow, there'd been no major complications so far.

At James's suggestion, she'd agreed to come down to the studio for the first take of *Friends*, the song she'd written for Frank. She'd also agreed to finally come forth as the songwriter, telling the other band members her well-kept secret. *Friends* was going to be a single cut from the album, as well as the album title.

She sat quietly, watching and waiting for the taping to start for the fifth time. She'd thought the first four had been flawless, but Frank and James each found something that didn't mesh. She found it amusing each time it was wrong someone did or said something totally off the wall and everyone burst into fits of laughter. It helped to ease the tension and frustration in the room, and she welcomed it.

For the fifth time, the tune came to an end as the last piano key was struck. James removed his headset. "Finally. Play it back."

Her entire being felt on fire. James stood next to the soundproof glass smiling at her, and then gave her a thumbs up and motioned for her to join them. *Whew! He believes this is it.*

The nerves under her skin quivered with anticipation when one of the engineers rewound the tape. She slipped past them and walked through the doors into James' waiting arms.

The engineer's voice came over the system. "We're ready to run the tape."

She sat next to Frank and waited along with James, the band, and everyone else. The soft, even sounds of the piano came through the speakers, followed by the accompanying instruments and vocals. The music purred through the air.

Heather closed her eyes. *It's so beautiful, soothing, and...* her thought unfinished, a chill shivered through her, leaving goose bumps on her flesh. Her words, Frank's melody, and James's voice were a perfect blend.

James slipped his arm around her shoulder, kissing and kissed her gently on the cheek as the final note played quietly. The tears welled up in her eyes, burst through the barrier, and streamed down her face. James kissed them away, and she smiled, knowing how lucky she was.

"Well..." James's tone was as serious as in the previous four recording attempts. He got up, leaving Heather feeling unprotected. "I don't know about the rest of you, but..." he said, his back to her and the rest of the band members. When he turned around, the smile covering his face chased away any fears she may have harbored. "I think that's a wrap. We got it!"

"WoooHooo!"

She stayed off to the side, taking in the merriment and everything else going on around her. She wanted to make sure every moment of this occasion was documented into her memory, something she could pull out to share with her children.

"Heather," James' soft, masculine voice eased its way into her daze, "we really should tell them now."

"Now?" she asked, focusing on his face for the strength seeping from her body. Was she really ready for the world to know she'd written those words? Wasn't this her dream when she came to Nashville?

"What better time? We've got to get the information for the album ready before printing. Then there's the cover to consider." James hesitated a moment, taking her hands into his. He caressed them softly with the tips of his fingers. "I've got an idea, if you want to hear it."

"Sure," she said, as quietly as she could.

"Okay. How does this sound?" James' inhaled deeply, pulling her off to the side, away from the bustle of the studio. "The scene is a field of wild flowers, the breeze fluttering across the field, the sky a soft, powder blue. In the field, a man and a woman are embraced in each other's arms. The woman's long hair is flowing in the breeze, obviously totally in love."

She had a feeling who he'd been picturing on that cover. "Sounds romantic, James. It has a soft, loving appeal to it. But do you think it's a big old fashioned?"

"Maybe. It's only an idea, and the artist will decide for sure. Now on to the other stuff."

He took her slightly trembling hand, led her back to the center of excitement, and waited for a brief pause in the nonstop chatter.

"Can I get a word or two in here?" James asked.

Heather squeezed his hand, not from pain, but from fright.

"I have something to tell everyone. As you all know, *Friends* came to us from Frank. Well, the melody, anyway." He moved slightly away from her, leaving her to face her fears on her own. "The lyrics, however, are from Heather."

She stood waiting for the onslaught of disapproval. Instead, she was smothered with hugs and kisses of congratulations. Her eyes moist, she searched for the safety of James's dark eyes. Nothing but pride and love, radiated in them.

They say the eyes are the doorway to one's soul. In this case, she believed it was true. Behind James's slightly opened curtain to his soul was a bounty of love for her, filling her heart with joy.

****

"Okay, let the woman breath," James laughed standing next to Heather, shielding her. *Will I always feel this way about her? Please don't let me ever resent any public attention she may get. I don't want to act like a fool or feel a twinge of jealousy. Me jealous of Heather? Never!*

"I agree, let's go celebrate." Frank's voice broke through the noise around them, helping to ease the attention bestowed upon Heather. "Tell ya what. Let's get something to eat and meet back at the club in a couple of hours. Oh yeah, it's on me."

"All right, let's go!"

"Thanks, buddy," James said, patting Frank on the shoulder. He'd been anxious for the session to end, and welcomed Frank's suggestion. He wanted to have some time alone with Heather. The session had been stressful, especially for someone who didn't have any idea what would happen.

The recording of the album had been a long and weary ordeal. He wanted nothing more than to erase the tension he felt in Heather's body and knew was present in his. The only way to do that was to get out of here for much-needed quality alone time.

Chapter Twenty-Four

Friends broke into the top ten on Billboard's country charts three weeks later. The sensible side of Heather kept her feet solidly on the ground. A wee little voice kept telling her one hit song didn't make a star. There was still a lot of hard work ahead of her; she'd have to prove she wasn't a one-hit wonder in the business. The next one might not even get in the top one-hundred.

James stood waiting for her outside the door. She made her way through the parking lot slowly, trying to chase away the tingling of her nerves. Or at least keep them under wraps. She didn't want any one, including James, knowing how scared she was about the whole deal.

"Hi, hon." James wrapped his arms around her. Her breasts pressed against him, his heartbeat in rhythm with hers.

"Hi," she said, looking into his eyes as his lips captured hers. She loved the way he kissed her— soft and slow, none of that sloppy and hurried stuff.

"Come on," he said, guiding her in to the bar.

She stepped through the doorway and into a world that changed overnight. She was a celebrity now, not a normal everyday person coming out for a good time. Or at least that's the way she thought everyone would treat her. It worried her a bit. She didn't want to be treated any differently. She was still the same old Heather.

Everyone she loved waited for her. Robert and Rona, Kathi and Frank, people from her job, and people she knew but weren't all that close with. Standing next to a table with a huge record-shaped cake on it was Will Sheridan and his wife of fifty-plus years. Heather could only stand in awe.

"Girl, you better close your mouth," Rona remarked, wrapping her arms around Heather. "It's hanging down on the floor."

"Oh." She snapped her jaw closed, feeling her cheeks warm slightly. "Thank God the lights are low," she whispered back to her cousin.

"Heather!"

Her attention was drawn to a group of girls waving their arms. Tears filled her eyes as she made her way over to five of her former co-workers from Wisconsin.

"When did you all get here? Kathi didn't say anything about anyone from home being here." She swallowed the raw emotional knot caught in her throat.

"We know," Judy said. "It was supposed to be a surprise. Everyone is soooo proud of you, Heather. You actually had the guts to follow your dream, something not one of us has the nerve to do."

"Thanks. I had some help," she said, pointing to James and Frank. "Without them, this may not even have happened."

"Yeah, well, it did."

The chit-chat went on for a few more minutes before she felt James come up behind her.

"Excuse me." James' deep sultry southern voice lulled the unsuspecting women into a brief goo-goo-eyed sphere. She couldn't help but smile at their reaction. "I hate to be the bad guy here, but I need to steal Heather away from you."

"Oh, okay." She took hold of James's hand. Before she could move an inch, she felt someone grab her arm.

"Heather, who is this hunk of southern hospitality?" Judy gushed, smiling like a woman hell-bent on having a good time.

Heather turned back to her friends. "This is James Sheridan, the man who sings the song. He's my best and closest friend." She slipped her arm around his waist, basking in the knowledge that she was his. "James, these are a few friends from Madison."

"Hi," James said, shaking each of their hands. "I hope your stay is enjoyable."

"If there's more like you around here, it's practically a guarantee," Barb cooed, holding on to his hand a bit longer than the three before her.

"I'll see what I can do," he proposed, winking as he kissed Heather on the cheek and then guided her away from her giggling friends.

He nudged her side. "You, my dear, have very flirty friends."

"It's your own fault," she teased back. "If you weren't so damn sexy, they wouldn't be over there wetting their panties."

"Say what!?" he said, slapping her on the rear. "By the way, you have a phone call." He reached over the bar, grabbing the receiver for her.

Who would be calling me? Everyone I know is here tonight.

"Hello?" she asked.

"Heather Jones?"

"Yes," she answered, covering her right ear to block out the noise around her.

"This is Samuel Mortinson from WSM-FM. I'd thought you'd like to know Billboard's new chart came out. *Friends* has debuted at number 4."

"What? What did you say?" she queried, straining to hear the local disc jockey. *No way I heard that right.* Reaching back for a chair to steady herself, she found James.

Samuel repeated the news, and she fell into James's lap. "Oh," she whispered, dropping the receiver on the bar. She gulped down a glass of water, trying to moisten the sudden dryness in her throat. *Holy shit!*

"James…" She turned into his arms. "We hit number four! Can you believe it? Number 4." She threw her arms around his neck, planting a kiss solidly on his lips. Then the trembling came, slight at first before making her feel cold as ice. Fear was settling in. "What if it's just a fluke? What if the next time the song's a total flop? What if…"

"Shhhhhh, don't worry about that right now. Let's just tell everyone the good news and get on with the party. We've got plenty of time to discuss it," James assured her.

His voice soothed her, but the fear was still very much alive in her. *New Love* was the next song scheduled to be debuted at Gabe's. She knew all about one-hit wonders and how those artists just faded away. She didn't want to be in that category of songwriters; she didn't want James and the boys to fall in that category, either.

****

"James," Heather asked, wondering if he'd go for her idea.

"Mmmm?" he said, reaching over to take her hand in his.

"Would you consider recording *New Love* regardless of how it does at Gabe's? I'm afraid the ball might stop rolling if we don't keep behind it," she suggested, hoping he'd see her reasoning. After all, why should they stop now? Even if *New Love* only made it in the top fifty, that was still a good showing, wasn't it?

James glanced quickly at her. "Sure, but why?"

She took a deep breath, letting it out slowly. "Oh, you know. To prove to myself I can do this. That I'm cut out to be a songwriter."

He chuckled lightly, squeezing her fingers. "Actually, I was going to ask you the same thing."

"Really?" she exclaimed, feeling the nervous beads on her brow dissipate. *I should have known. Worry wart that I am.* "With the same conditions?"

James pulled into her driveway and around to the backdoor. "I wouldn't have it any other way. Why fix something that's not broke?"

He captured her lips in a deep, mind-blowing kiss before releasing her hand and looking out the windshield. "We'll talk about it later. We both need some sleep." He fidgeted a bit, but didn't look at or touch her again. "Don't worry, Heather. Frank's been working on the song for a while; it won't take much to get it ready. In fact, I think maybe we can do a test run tonight…if you're up to it."

"Sure," she said, sliding out of the car.

****

Heather's image in his rearview mirror haunted James. She'd looked defeated, rejected and used…like an old toy. Boy, was she wrong. He'd had something important to ask her, but he'd lost his nerve. Especially after she'd asked about the next song. The timing just wasn't right. Destiny had stepped between them, forcing him to wait for another opportunity.

He flipped open his cell phone, punching Frank's preprogrammed number.

"This better be good," Frank said, sleep dripping in his voice.

"Just listen. Tonight we're going to introduce *New Love* at the club. I'll fill you in later today. Later." James closed the phone, cutting off the call. He'd never been afraid of anything in his life, except getting married again. Now he couldn't wait to do it again, if she'd have him.

Chapter Twenty-Five

Two years later….

Heather's songwriter career skyrocketed after *New Love* landed in the number three slot on the Billboard charts. The winter and spring tours had been a huge success. She and James sealed their deal permanently with a wedding ring and God's blessing.

All her dreams had come true. She'd been validated as a talented songwriter, having hit after hit on the charts. Of course, she had James and Frank to thank for that. If not for their talents, she'd still be working at the Ramada, happy as a lark. Although, a CMA nomination next year would be the frosting on the cake for them all.

Tingles of excitement flowed through her as she waited for the plane to taxi to a complete stop. She felt like a long-lost friend returning, instead of the complete stranger she'd been the first time she'd come to the city.

On this early October evening, the air hung onto the warmth of the day. Kathi, not Rona, would be meeting her this time around. She was anxious to see her friend again. Kathi and Frank had been married shortly before she and James had moved back to Wisconsin. They'd kept his Nashville house on the hill where Utah and his lovely bride, Emerald, kept house when in town. Even though James found he enjoyed the mounds of snow living up North offered during the winter months, Heather knew he longed to return to his hilltop home. He didn't even seem to mind the bitter cold nights, as long as the two of them were cuddled up in front of the fireplace.

These days, James was on the road a lot, like now, and their time together was probably better than if they'd spent every day together. They'd come to value that time with only minor disagreements circling around the newest song. Their marriage was one made in Heaven, peaceful and loving.

Heather scanned the baggage claim area as she stepped off the escalator. "Kathi!" she cried, trotting over to the friend who was more like a sister.

"Hey, let me at least breath," Kathi laughed, hugging Heather just as tightly.

"Any word from Frank?" Heather inquired, breaking her hold then heading toward the luggage.

"None," Kathi muttered, loneliness edging the single word.

Heather knew exactly how she felt. She'd been feeling empty since James had left for Montana. This trip worried her. This time of year, the weather in the mountains was unpredictable.

Grabbing her bags, she and Kathi headed toward the exit doors. "What the hell is this?" she asked, eyeing the black stretch limo and driver holding the door open for them. *Leave it to Kathi.*

"I thought you'd like to ride a Thoroughbred back to your house," Kathi said, climbing into the backseat.

Heather followed her, smiling at the driver as he closed the door. She'd never been in a limo before, and wasn't sure she'd really like it. But the thought was a sweet one, and she loved Kathi for it.

"Heather, it's been two years since you've been back here. Why not stay this time?" Kathi poured them each a glass of champagne and then handed one to her. "Or at least use it for a summer home. You can always use the house in Wisconsin during the winter, since you both like the snow so much."

"I don't know. I hate leaving the horses for any length of time, you know. Let's discuss it later," she offered, sipping the champagne and thinking of James. "James said last week the plane was due in the afternoon following their last show. I hope the weather holds out and they get back here safe and sound."

"You are such a worry wart. It's a couple of days away, so just relax while you're here and have fun," Kathi said.

Relax. Like I can relax after the dream last night. Something's not right. I just hope I'm wrong. She'd never worried about James being out on the road as much as she had this time around. She'd woken in the middle of the night, her gown soaked with sweat. The plane carrying the band had gone done in Montana in an unexpected blizzard.

She shook off the dread as the limo came to a stop behind their Nashville home. From the looks of it, Frank and Kathi were taking good care of the place in absence of the Sheridan men. Once outside the iron carriage, she walked slowly around to the front of the home, stopping at the very spot where she and James had almost made love for the first time. Warmth spread through her as she recalled the sweet memory.

James, please come back to me safe and sound. Please let the dream be just that, a dream, she prayed, and then walked back to where Kathi stood waiting for her.

After two years, James's presence still filled the home, and his scent filled every pore of her body. *This is your home, darlin'*, she heard him say as if he stood next to her.

"Come on, Heather, put those bags down. Go upstairs, grab a pair of jeans, a clean shirt, and let's go," Kathi urged, already heading up the stairs.

"Go where, Kathi? I just got here," she called, lugging her suitcases up one step at a time until she reached the master bedroom.

"Anywhere; we've got to pass the time by doing something other than just sitting around here." Kathi was already in the room, waiting for Heather to flip her cases up on the bed.

"Hey!" Heather cried out. Evidently, she wasn't moving fast enough; Kathi pulled a case out of her hand, plopped it on the bed, then withdrew some clothes from it. Heather caught the clothing as it was tossed at her, a pair of boots following the jeans and shirt in her arms.

"Now, go! You wanna see Rona, don't you?" Kathi blurted, strutting out of the room like a peacock.

****

"Hey! You were the one in such a big hurry. Let's go," Heather teased, bounding down the stairs finding Kathi sitting back in an easy chair with her eyes closed. "People to see, you know."

"What took you so long, anyway?" Kathi teased, stretching out of the chair. Reaching the door, she pulled it open and bowed at the waist. "Your buggy awaits."

Heather shook her head, and then glided through the door, coming to a complete stop before her second step hit the ground. "Where's the limo?" Parked in the drive was Frank's beat-up old van. "You mean to tell me you two still drive around in that beast?"

"Hey, don't look at me. Just get in, and let's go without another word about Frank's pride and joy," Kathi instructed, closing the door behind her.

"Geez, no one would suspect anyone of importance would be in this thing." Heather laughed, yanking open the passenger door.

Kathi climbed into the driver's seat, giggling at the squeaking door hinges. "Exactly Frank's feelings."

Putting the van into gear, Kathi edged the bucket of rust down the drive and onto Dickerson.

"Rona said they'd be staying at the Ramada. We'll stop by there first."

"Good. A nice quiet reunion before going to Gabe's." Heather looked out the window, watching the buildings pass by in a foggy gaze. "I wonder if any of the old crowd is still around."

Kathi just smiled and kept her eyes on the road. Heather sat back, enjoying what she saw of the city that had been as familiar to her as breathing. Everything, yet nothing, changed. Time and absence played on her emotions. How could she have left this town and all her friends? She'd loved Nashville and the life it had not only offered her, but given her beyond her wildest dreams.

Heather had arrived in town with a pipe dream every other dreamer had…to be part of the country music business, whether as an artist or a songwriter. Thankfully, Frank and James had taken her seriously. If they hadn't, none of them would be where they were today with a couple of hit songs and marriages they'd only dreamt of.

"That's their room right there. Ya ready?" Kathi asked, pulling Heather from her bittersweet memories.

Getting out of the van, they went over the door of Rona's hotel room. "There don't seem to be any lights on, Kathi. I don't think they're here," Heather declared, trying to peer through the slight opening in the curtains.

"Yeah, I talked to them the other night. They knew you were coming today," Kathi said, stepping away from the door. "I bet they're at Gabe's."

Heather walked towards the back of the hotel, "You coming?" She waved for Kathi to follow her to the back and through the small opening in the trees. Just beyond that tree line was Gabe's. A sense of high energy quickened her pace when she saw the club lights flickering through the branches. Every new song she'd ever written had been, introduced there, and still was.

"They got a new sign and the name's spelled differently," Heather noted, slipping through the trees. Shaking her head, she continued across the browned grass until she reached the patio.

Pausing for a moment, she slid open the doors and peered inside. Where once there were video games now stood more tables and chairs. The smell of grilling food brought to mind how hungry she was.

Stepping down the few steps to the main bar, which had been moved from one wall to another, she couldn't believe the changes. New lights, carpet, paneling on the wall. Wow! The place had been spruced up, to say the least. Even with the new changes, the old smells and feeling of the old Gabe's lingered. She doubted anything would ever change that.

"The usual, Darlin'?" The question followed the sound of a glass on the bar.

"Janey!" Heather cried, reaching across the bar to give an old friend a big hug.

As if on cue, everyone who'd touched her life in Nashville materialized out of thin air. They welcomed her back home. James's home.

James, I wish you were here with me. In a few days, you will be, and I'll never let you leave without me again. I love you and miss you so much, Heather thought, feeling his absence in her heart.

The party went on rather uneventfully, much to Heather's pleasure. She didn't want to face any questions about a possible CMA nomination for *Whispering Wind*. The song could conceivably receive three nominations in the video, song of the year, and songwriter of the year categories. It had been the sixth Top Ten hit for them in the past two years.

Success had found them, and she worked hard to make sure nothing caused it to loosen its grip on her and the people she loved.

****

Heather sat at the bar alone, eating a hot ham and Swiss. With the dinner hour upon them, the party-goers vacated to fill their bellies. They'd agreed to all return before the house band started up for the night.

"It's hard to believe this is where it all turned around."

She turned, looking into Robert's caring eyes. "It sure is," she agreed, scanning the near empty room. Empty or not, she pictured the night *Friends* had been first introduced. It had been the most exciting night of her life, well that and the night James had finally gotten up the nerve to ask her to marry him. "What would I have done without everyone? And without James, my life wouldn't be complete."

"The magic's still there?" Robert asked, his smile reflected in his bright eyes.

"Always. I'm as much in love with him now as I was the first time I laid eyes on his face," she said, wishing he were there with her now.

One show tonight and on the plane tomorrow morning. A few hours in the air, non-stop, and you'll be in my arms again. Darlin', I miss you so much.

Chapter Twenty-Six

James sat in his hotel room in the town of their final stop on the tour. He couldn't wait to get home, back to Nashville where his beloved Heather waited for him. He'd been away only three months this time, but time and loneliness made it feel like an eternity.

One show tonight and board a plane late tomorrow morning. A few hours in the air, and you'll be in my arms again, Heather. I miss you so much.

This last leg of the tour took James and the boys into the ranges of Billings, Montana. He'd had enough of mountain passes and open land to fill him a lifetime. He wanted to go home, home to Heather.

Why wait for a plane, crowded airport, security, and possible delays? Picking up the phone, he dialed Frank's room.

"Hello."

"Frank, is everyone ready?" James tossed clothes into his one of his bags.

"Yeah."

"Have everyone pack their stuff," he instructed, not waiting another second. He needed to get home. The sooner, the better.

"Why?"

"'Cuz we're going to head back right after the show. We've all been away too long from our families." James snapped shut the suitcase and then reached for his duffle bag. "And I'm in no mood to deal with the hassle of being at the airport."

"Eeee Ha! You serious?"

"Serious as a heart attack. Get those guys movin'; we're due at the arena in half an hour."

"You got it, boss. I can't wait to call Kathi and…"

"No! I want it to be a surprise." James said, running a hand through his hair. "Understand?"

"Okay." Disappointment clearly filled Frank's voice, yet James knew he'd do as he asked.

Heather, honey, I'm on my way home. James put down the receiver, then busied himself with packing the remainder of his belongings.

Zipping the duffle shut, he grabbed his jacket, picked up the baggage, and walked out the door, turning out the light behind him.

****

James and the boys had to practically run into the Billings auditorium and their dressing rooms. The mob of people outside had been waiting hours to get a piece of them to take home as souvenirs. All he wanted to worry about was getting the show done and on the road no later than ten o'clock…if possible. If he had to cut the show short, he would. At this point, he didn't care what a promoter might say or do.

This was no time for the jitters. The only thing on everyone's mind…going home. He'd told his band mates they'd do a two-and-a-half-hour show and head off the stage for good no later than ten o'clock.

Reaching the darkness of the stage, the band slipped into position. The lights came up slowly and James gave the signal for the introductory two-step number. Moving closer to the microphone, he waved out to the screaming crowd.

"Hellooooo Billings! Are you ready for a good time tonight?" he yelled into the microphone. The crowd roared louder and rowdier. "All right, then…let's party!"

****

The Night Ramblers finished up their last encore and finally loaded up the tour bus by ten-thirty. With the road crew being delayed by a few hours, James decided not to wait for them. His desire to get home grew stronger with each passing moment, and nothing was going to stand in his way of getting there.

If they took turns driving, they would be back to Nashville in about twenty-four hours. Even though realistically, they'd be home tomorrow night if he'd only been patient and waited to fly out in the morning. No, he wanted to feel like he was doing something to get there, not sitting around in a cold hotel room. He missed his wife.

A light snow fell as the last man climbed aboard the bus. James shut the door, turned on the windshield wipers, and eased out of the parking lot onto the road. By the time they'd reached the city limits, the white powdery snow increased. It was melting as soon as it hit the ground; he had a feeling it wouldn't be long before the temp would drop, and the pavement took on the white blanket of winter. He also knew, having spent a few winters in Wisconsin, he was the one better equipped to drive in it.

Before long, the only noise in the bus was the humming of the heater and the snores of the men sleeping behind him. The driving conditions along Interstate 90 grew increasingly worse. A light film of ice covered the roads. He worried what the conditions would be like the farther they got into the mountains.

"Me and my blasted big ideas. I should have just waited," He muttered to himself, concentrating on the road so hard he didn't see the deer until the last moment. Trying to bring the bus to a safe stop, he slid on a patch of snow-covered ice and lost control of the vehicle. The motor-home-styled bus slid off the pavement skating in a ravine. He briefly saw the grove of trees before his head smashed against the steering wheel. Then all was dark and silent.

****

"Ouch! Oooooooo," James lifted his head from the steering wheel and opened his eyes to a windshield full of pine tree limbs. A lump the size of a goose egg throbbed relentlessly on his forehead.

Slowly, he slid out of the seat. "Frank? Frank!" he called out, moving up a small incline toward the back of the bus. He paused and checked the other men as he did so, wrapping blankets around them as much as he could.

There was a gash above Frank's left eye. Finding the first aid kit, James cleaned up the blood seeping out of the wound.

"Frank, wake up," he said, shaking him gently. Reaching over for another blanket, he tucked it around Frank's body, then checked and rechecked the other band members.

"Okay, I'm gonna try to get some help. The blankets should keep you warm until I get back," he said, more for himself then for his unconscious friends. Walking to the front of the bus, he picked up his heavy winter coat, hat, and gloves. "The ignition is off. I'd better check for any gas leak."

Pushing through the doors, he immediately shoved them until they closed. The temperature had dropped several degrees. He knew the wind that had picked up made it feel colder than it really was, not that it wasn't cold enough. Wind chill factor, one of the things he'd learned about living in Wisconsin. A man could get frost bit in a matter of seconds if he wasn't careful.

Trudging through the snow, he checked every inch of the bus for damage or leaks of any kind. Once he'd finished his second round, he climbed back into the vehicle. He estimated he'd been outside for about ten minutes. In that time, it seemed colder and windier than when he'd first stepped out. He needed an extra blanket to wrap around himself to keep warm as the temperature inside the bus dropped. He doubled checked his band mates, throwing anything on them that would keep the heat in their bodies.

Pushing through the doors again, he stepped into the frigid night. A blanket around his shoulders, he searched for the tire marks leading back to the highway. He'd had no idea the bus slid quite a distance before coming to rest in the trees.

He plowed through the snow for over an hour before conceding he had no idea where he was or in what direction he'd been going. It was much colder, and the snow fell heavier with each step he'd taken. *I'm lost, damn it.*

He pulled the blanket closer to him, hoping it was enough with the coat to keep him warm. Peering through the snow, he spotted some trees and headed for them. He might be able to find some kind of shelter there from the storm. Hopefully, he'd find some way of building a fire to keep warm until daylight.

In snow knee-deep now, James put all his dwindling strength into reaching the pine trees. He paused a moment to catch his breath and survey his surroundings. The grove stood only a few feet in front of him, with a beautiful thirty-footer nestled in the middle.

Crawling under the tree, he huddled next to the trunk and pulled the blanket closer around his face. Sleep overtook his shivering body as thoughts of Heather warmed his mind and soul.

Chapter Twenty-Seven

Heather and Kathi were among the last to leave Gabe's. After a bottle of champagne, Heather found it hard to keep her eyes open any longer, and had finally talked Kathi into going home.

Silence filled the drive back to the house. Heather's mind filled with all sort of things. Being back in town only made her realize how homesick she was. Maybe that was why she'd stayed away for two years. She hadn't wanted to face the reality that home was here, in Nashville.

"Kathi?" She looked across the seat to her friend, a friend who'd become more of a sister over the years.

"Yeah?"

"I think I'm going to talk to James about selling the house." she wished she could see the expression on Kathi's face. *I bet her eyes are bugging out of her head!*

"House… What house?" Suspicion edged Kathi's question, making Heather smile in the darkness of the van.

"You know…*the* house." She looked away, fearing she'd burst out laughing if she saw Kathi's expression.

"Not the one here, I hope."

"Of course not, silly." She reached over, punching Kathi in the arm. "Being back here again made me realize how much this place means to me."

Kathi pulled up alongside the Sheridan home then turned off the ignition. "Well, that's a relief. Just give us enough time to find a place, though, okay? And there's Utah and Emerald to think about."

"Deal." Heather said sliding out of the van. She walked up to the back door, fumbling in her purse for her unused set of house keys. "I think they've already found their dream home. James has been talking for hours at a time with his little brother lately.

"And there's really nothing to keep us up north. My family's scattered, and James's is right here," she said, walking from the entryway to the living room. Tossing a couple of logs into the fireplace, only a few moments passed before a warm fire began to roar. "Besides, I'd like our baby to be raised here."

"Your what?" Kathi exclaimed, leaning toward her.

"Now don't get excited. I'm thinking of the future, that's all." Heather pulled a blanket up around her, savoring the warm feeling of being home.

"How far into the future, Heather?" Kathi asked.

"Not far," she said, absent-mindedly poking the small burning logs. *We're finally having the child we've longed for, James.*

****

"James!" Heather cried out from her sleep. She sprung up, catching her breath and holding a hand to her chest.

"Heather, what is it?" Kathi ran to her side, taking hold of her by the shoulders. "You're shaking like a leaf."

"I…I don't know," Heather said, slowly shaking her head. "James—something's happened to James. Kathi, something terri…" she started, sniffing her nose and wiping at the burning tears slipping from her eyes.

"Sh-sh-sh, it was only a dream," Kathi cooed, handing her a tissue. "Go back to sleep."

"No, I can feel it. Something's gone wrong," Heather replied, reaching for the safety of the Navajo blanket.

"Heather, everything's okay. Nothing has happened to James or anyone else," Kathi promised, returning to the comfort of the sofa she'd been curled up on. "Try to get some sleep."

Sleep? Anything but. Heather wrapped the blanket tightly around her, rocking gently to and fro. She trembled as if the window were open on a brisk winter night. Something was definitely wrong, she just couldn't put her finger on it. All she could see was James, and the last time they were together as truly being their last time together.

****

Heather was coaxed out of her restless sleep by the persistent ringing of the cell phone. The mid-morning sun peeked through the curtains as she got up from the pillows on the floor. Reaching the phone, she swiped the screen in haste.

"Hello," she yawned into the phone. "Excuse me. Yes, this is Heather Sheridan."

Her mind raced like a speeding car as she listened to the all-too-formal voice. Icy fear twisted around her heart, and the phone slipped from her sweaty palms. At that very moment, she ceased to exist. She felt about as alive as an ant who'd just been squashed.

"Hello, this is Kathi Whitman. May I help you?"

Heather felt someone take her hand, squeezing it lightly. Kathi… Was that Kathi's voice in the distance?

"Who is this?" she asked, putting the cell on speaker.

"My name is Deputy Sheriff Fuller of the Montana State Patrol. Your husband and three other men were found inside a bus. They went off an icy road and…"

Sheriff? Montana? Heather's mind registered little of the voice coming over the phone, but enough to bring her out of her daze. She gently squeezed Kathi's hand, hoping it wasn't what she'd feared last night.

Kathi stared at her, listening to the sheriff. "My husband. Is he all right?"

"Yes, he's at St. Vincent's Hospital in Billings. He sustained a contusion over his left eye, and exposure."

Heather swallowed, closing her eyes. "James Sheridan… Is he all right?"

"I'm sorry, of the four men we found, none of them had any identification with that name on it. Mrs. Whitman, can we expect you to arrive soon?"

"Yes, as soon as we can get a flight out. Thank you for calling, Sheriff Fuller," Heather interjected then disconnected the call. "Where's James, Kathi? He wouldn't let those guys go out in bad weather."

She felt herself being guided across the room. "James will be found. He's strong. He'll survive. You have to believe that, Heather," Kathi encouraged, sitting on the arm of the chair next to Heather.

A deep breath escaped Heather as quickly as it had been trapped. Swallowing with difficulty, she found her voice realizing what they had to do…pleasant or not.

"We've got to pack. Call the airport and see when the next flight leaves for Billings." Heather walked with calculated steps, turning briefly to Kathi.

She sprinted up the stairs. All the fuses in her body were being blown all at once. The shaking wouldn't stop, and her mind raced a-hundred-miles-a-second. She had to stay in control. James was missing, and she'd need all her strength to keep herself from getting lost along with him.

Snapping the hurriedly packed suitcase shut, she swiped at the tears streaming down her cheeks.

Hold on, James, I'll be there as soon as I can. God, please let him be found alive!

Chapter Twenty-Eight

James woke stiff and cramped in the same position in which he'd fallen asleep. His cheeks burned, and his joints ached when he stretched out his legs. Rubbing them up and down, he hoped to get the blood moving a bit before trying to use them.

Satisfied with his efforts, he crawled out from under the tree until he could stand. He walked to the edge of the tree line, his tracks from the night before nothing but a memory. The sun burned brightly overhead, reflecting off the snow covered ground like a lake of diamonds.

"Late morning?" he guessed, shielding his eyes from the blinding sun. "Now let's see, I came from that way," he said half-aloud, looking in the direction he thought he'd come from the night before. "Or did I? Damn!" He turned, moving northeast, the opposite direction of the bus crash.

Snowcapped peaks of the Rocky Mountains. Trees were flocked in white powder and alive with birds and squirrels hidden safely among the branches and their needles. The terrain in front of him reflected fresh and white. Pure, like a baby's bottom or an inexperienced young lady. The non-polluted mountain air fresh and crisp. He took in deep breaths, wanting to capture the purity and beauty of it forever.

He plodded through the knee-deep snow, catching a glimpse of a doe and her fawn rushing off from the safety of the trees. The call of a hawk soaring overhead reminded him of nature's checks and balances. The graceful predator swooped down, successfully capturing a rabbit in its talons.

James watched in awe, listening to the low rumble of his own stomach. It had been well over twenty-four hours since he'd eaten anything solid; snow didn't count in the solid category.

The hawk soaring above wasn't the only predator on the prowl. Among the shadows of a tree line several yards in front of him, a mountain lion watched with interest. He'd been calculating each move James made, keeping them fresh in his predatory mind before moving in on his intended prey.

James kept plowing through the snow as the sun moved above him, signaling it should be high noon. *Heather, my love. Have the boys been found yet? Have you been told about the accident? As soon as the search party finds me, I'll be holding you close to me, never to let go again.*

He kept his mind focused on Heather and the wonderful warmth of her body next to his. Caught up in sexual desire, he heard the growl too late and felt himself plunge to the ground.

Man and cat wrestled for position on the snow packed ground. Using all his strength, James did what he could to keep the jaws of death from reaching him. He felt and heard his flesh tearing as the cat's thick sharp claws ripped through his layers of clothing.

The next few minutes hung suspended in time. James thought he'd surely died when a loud blast echoed through the trees and the monstrous cat fell still on his chest.

James's weakened breath and strength left his body. With the cat's dead body on top of him, darkness pulled him down into its void.

****

The warmth of a cracking cabin fire and the smell of stew brewing over the flames pulled James from the darkness. His coat and flannel shirt had been stripped away from his body. His arm and chest wounds were dressed and bandaged by someone who obviously knew what they'd been doing. An old tattered fur skin covered the bottom half of his body.

The cabin appeared to be large, housing a bed, table and chairs on the floor space. Judging by the heads hung on the walls and the bearskin rug on the floor in front of the fireplace, the owner was clearly an expert hunter.

"Aghhh," he groaned, lifting his body from the makeshift bed. Swinging his legs out from under the animal skin, he stood slightly hunched over. Stumbling over to the fireplace, he leaned on the mantel trying to straighten up while recalling what had happened.

A shot of cold air covered his body. He turned, finding the door wide open and a man as big as Grizzly Adams in the doorway. Snow and wind howled around the massive figure as he shut the door, shaking the snow from his furry hat.

"See ya woke up," the deep raspy voice said. "Been waitin' for ya to com 'round." He shed himself of the bearskin coat then sauntered over to James. "Stew's 'bout ready. Ya must be hungry."

James held his ground, his senses telling him he had nothing to fear. "Smells good. What's in it?" he asked, seeing the compassion in the man's chestnut brown eyes.

The man walked over to the pot, stirring its contents several times. "Little of this, little of that," he said, bringing a spoonful to his mouth, smacking his lips in satisfaction.

Feeling a bit dizzy, James made his way over to the wooden table. "Feel a little weak," he whispered, sitting on a chair made from a tree trunk.

"Should be; that cat took a lot out of ya," the man said, spooning the stew into a couple of roughly carved wooden bowls. "Never seen nothin' like it. Good thing you're a healthy man. The wounds ain't so bad. That heavy city-made coat helped ya there."

He set a bowl and spoon in front of James before taking the chair opposite him. James watch the man who'd taken him in, cared for him, not knowing what else to do.

"Mister, ya better eat. Need to get your strength up." The man slurped between spoonfuls of stew. "Been out for about three days now. Ya was mumblin' something, couldn't make it out though."

James brought his hand up to his chin, only to pull it back in shock at the growth he touched. "Three days... I've been out for three days?" He shook in disbelief. It couldn't be possible. Wasn't someone out looking for him by now?

"Do ya 'member what happened," his host asked.

"Up to the part of fightin' with that cat and then hearing some sort of blast," James remembered, trying to come to terms with the passage of time.

"That was me."

"You?"

"I came over the ridge just as he leaped at ya. I was out of gun range so all I could do was run 'til I could get a clear shot. Been tracking that cat fer days," the man said, pride flittering across his face.

James took into account what the stranger continued to tell him. When the end finally came, it dawned on him just what the guy was saying.

"Three days. I've got to get back...my wife. She'll be going out of her mind by now," James said, his voice low and filled with concern.

"Believe so, but ya ain't goin' nowhere. Ya ain't healed properly yet for such a trip through this here country. End up dying' and all my good doctorin' fer nothin'."

"How soon, then?" James asked, the pain in his body reminding him of his wounds. Every muscle ached and he felt lightheaded like he'd just gotten off a carnival ride.

"Week, maybe. If the weather holds up."

"My name's James." James offered his hand in friendship. "And you are?"

"Buck, just Buck."

"Well, Buck, I owe you my life, it would seem," James said, his hand dwarfed inside Buck's. He spooned the rest of the oddly delicious stew into his mouth.

"Naw, ferget it," Buck said, wiping the back of his hand across his mouth.

"By the way, this is pretty good," James commented, smiling up at Buck. "What kind of meat is in it?"

"Three-day-old mountain lion." Buck laughed, getting up from the table. James abruptly stopped licking his lips, spewing the food across the table laughing smile softened Buck's face. Breaking stride, he stood, still cocking his head toward the door. The howl of the cold wind violently circled the cabin. "Storm brewin'…a bad one."

"It's just the wind," James said, feeling his stomach gurgle.

"Canadian wind, the worst. Could be held up here fer days. Won't be fit for man nor beast out there."

A shiver tore through James, as he realized he'd be stuck in a cabin in the middle of God's country for the time being.

Chapter Twenty-Nine

The flight into Billings had been a long and quiet one. Heather had imagined at least a hundred different situations James could be in. He could be frozen to death. He could be wandering aimlessly through the mountain range. At least Kathi knew Frank was alive, she didn't even have that little morsel to go on. She only knew James hadn't been found with the wreckage and a search party had been formed. Other than that, she was in the dark.

A car and police escort waited for them as they departed the plane. What little luggage they'd brought with them was tossed in to the trunk of the black car. Heather felt thousands of eyes watching her. Rolling up the window, she welcomed the dark panes that shut out the outside world.

The driver took them straight to the hospital; the police station would wait until morning. Gently, Heather put an arm around Kathi's shoulder. She'd hadn't realized what this was doing to her friend. She'd been filled with her own grief. Tears flowed down her cheeks, finally feeling the sorrow Kathi tried to hide.

"Heather?" Kathi's small, weak voice broke through the thick silence.

"Um?" Heather looked at her friend, amazed at her strength.

"Thanks."

"For what?"

"Being here." Kathi squeezed Heather's hand. "James will be found. I just know it. Don't worry."

"Easier said than done." Heather flashed a false half smile. She felt anything but strong and confident they'd find him. "I know you're right." *Why can't James be lying in a hospital bed waiting for me? Maybe the police have found him and they haven't been able to reach me. Maybe Frank will have some answers he hasn't told anyone else.*

Hope and faith—that was all she had to hold on to for the moment. A deep sigh escaped from somewhere inside and her gazed returned to the unseen sights passing by the window.

The car finally pulled up to the front door of the hospital. The sanitary smell of the medical facility overwhelmed her as they were escorted into the hospital. A nauseous feeling settled in the pit of her stomach as they approached the nurse's station.

"Excuse me," Kathi said, her voice barely audible. Heather put her arm around her, feeling her tremble. She wished she could take away the pain, but she couldn't. It was out of her hands.

"Yes?" a starchy-looking woman of around sixty said.

"Could you please tell me what room Frank Whitman's in, please?"

"Whitman, Frank Whitman." The woman's skilled fingers ran through the registry with ease. "Ah, yes, Frank Whitman. I'm sorry, miss, he's not allowed any visitors. Only his wife and another woman is listed here."

"Yes, Kathi Whitman. That's me. I'm his wife," Kathi said. Heather felt jealous of her happiness. It was silly, she should feel happiness. How could she when her husband was lost somewhere in the middle of no man's land fighting for his life?

Looking for confirmation from the attending officer, the nurse gave Kathi the room number. Heather started following Kathi as she practically ran down the hall.

"Only his wife, miss."

Heather froze, knowing in her heart she had to be the other name on the list. "Is Heather Sheridan listed?"

"Yes."

"I'm Heather Sheridan. Kathi wait," she yelled, jogging after her friend.

****

Heather stood in the doorway, watching Kathi shower Frank with kisses. A tear slid from the corner of her eye. *Oh, James, where are you?*

"Heather, how ya doin'?" Frank barely whispered, pain edging his voice.

"I'm okay, but how are you?" She asked, walking over to the bed and taking Frank's hand in hers for support.

"Okay, just a cut and exposure. Could have been worse, though," he reasoned, his bruised eyes looking her over as if it were her lying in that bed and not him. "Any word on James?"

Heather hung her head, steeling herself against the wave of emotion. "No, not that I know of. What the hell happened out there, Frank?"

"I don't really know. The last thing I remember, James was driving," Frank explained. "Next thing I knew, I was in an ambulance. James was nowhere to be found."

Heather walked over to the lone window, a deep, exhausted sigh escaping from somewhere in her. Pushing the curtain aside, she stared out at the dark outline of the distant mountain range. Something out there called softly to her. A chill rang through her body, and the curtain slipped back into place.

Chapter Thirty

Heather stood in her hotel room, throwing accusations at Frank. "Don't you understand I can't leave without knowing?"

"Heather…" Frank shuffled toward her. She shrunk away from his outreached arms. She couldn't stand to look at the pity in his eyes, let alone feel it in his touch.

"Don't touch me," Heather bellowed, backing away from him.

Frank stopped dead in his tracks, the look on his face a mixture of dismay and pity. "Let's be reasonable here, Heather. They've been searching for weeks now. The weather's become a factor here." He reached out for her again. "Nothing more can be done until the weather lets up. You know that. Even Utah has returned to Nashville to prepare the family for …"

"For what, death?" Whirling around, she landed right in Frank's outstretched arms. Surrounded by the comfort and warmth of his friendship, Heather broke down into long overdue weeping,

"Frank," she cried, sniffing as she looked into Frank's face. "I can't go on without James. He's my heart and soul," she whimpered, burying her head into his shoulder.

"Sh, sh, let it out, darlin'," he soothed, holding her and lightly stroking her tangled hair. "You've got to get some rest; you haven't slept since you got here. You'll be no good to James when they find him if you're weak and exhausted."

He guided her over to the bed, settling her down. She knew he was right. She wasn't making sense to herself, let alone to the people who knew her.

"Okay, Frank," she agreed, curling up into a ball. Once she relaxed, sleep swept over her in a matter of moments.

Chapter Thirty-One

Thanksgiving had come and gone. It had been hard enough for Heather to get through with James missing, and now Christmas closed in. Kathi wasn't sure how Heather would handle it. Her friend's appearance showed its neglect. She continuously lost weight, and her once-lustrous hair now hung dull from being unkempt. Lack of sleep showed itself in the grey lines under her eyes.

Kathi worried endlessly about Heather. She'd sit around the house with the only real communication being with the Montana state police, with the results being the same. The snow was too deep to send out a search party. The helicopters couldn't find any trace of a human in the mountain range. If James was dead, his body wouldn't be found until spring unless there was an unexpected thaw, which was unlikely this time of year.

Kathi stood in the doorway, Frank behind her with a Christmas tree in tow. "This has got to stop, Frank," Kathi said, her body trembling with fear for her friend. "She's just sinking deeper into depression."

"Maybe once we get the tree up and decorated, she'll start to come around," Frank suggested, pulling the tree past her and into the living room. "Nothing like Christmas to lift someone's spirits."

"I hope you're right," Kathi said, turning down the stereo playing one of James's albums for the thousandth time.

Heather remained curled up on the couch, wrapped up in James's old Navajo blanket. Kathi glanced over at her as she helped Frank right the six-foot blue spruce. Heather's empty eyes stared determinedly at the phone, as if willing it to come to life.

The room filled with the fresh scent of pine. Frank strung lights around the tree, and Kathi followed up with the boxes of ornaments they'd bought. Frank finished with the lights, then plugged them in. Heather continued to stare at the phone; she seemed to hardly breathe at all.

"Heather," Frank said, trying to break through her invisible force field.

"Heather, honey." He looked over at Kathi, his eyes begging her for help.

"Enough is enough." Kathi marched over to the stereo and opened it. After only a moment's hesitation, she took the needle from the groove in the record and purposely dropped it across the top of it.

"What the hell are you doing?!" The words struck out from Heather. Kathi stared at her, shocked, as Heather got up off the couch and stormed over to her. "I asked you what you think you're doing!" she continued to scream like a mad woman.

"Heather." Kathi's voice cracked with emotion, and she threw her arms around her long-lost friend. "I...I don't believe it."

"WHY did you do that, scratch the record? Why, Kathi, why" Heather sobbed, tears flowing down her cheeks for the first time since returning from Montana. She shoved Kathi away from her and then sank to the floor in front of the stereo, rocking back and forth.

At last the barrier was broken by something as simple as putting the songs of James to rest.

Taking Heather in his arms, Frank gently lifted and guided her back to the couch where he continued to hold her. She just kept rocking and asking Kathi why she'd done what she'd done. Kathi wanted to reach out and comfort her like a mother, but knew Heather needed to let it all out. All the fear she'd harbored for the past several months was bursting from its prison inside her. After a time, she finally fell asleep from exhaustion in Frank's arms.

Frank carried her up to her room. Kathi softly covered her with a blanket once Frank put her down.

"She'll sleep for a while now," Kathi said, closing the door behind them. Arm in arm, they walked backed down the stairs.

"I'm not going to leave her alone tonight, Frank," Kathi said, going through the pile of mail on the desk.

"*We're* not leaving her alone," he corrected, holding her close to him. Kathi absorbed as much of his strength as he'd give, it was one of the best parts of him. "She needs us more than ever now, Kathi. It's not going to be easy, but we'll make it happen."

"I know, it's just that," Kathi whispered, turning in his arms.

"Reality is something hard to face, for anyone. Don't worry, we'll be there if she stumbles," he assured her.

"I love you, Frank," she said and gathered his mouth with her own. She leaned her head against his chest and closed her eyes for a few moments. Taking a deep breath, she opened them and continued shuffling through the envelopes clustered in her hand.

"Another past due bill," she sighed, placing the notice from the utility company in the "to pay" pile.

"We'll have to take care of that," Frank said, returning to the tree and checking out their work. "Ya gonna help me some more with this or not?"

"Yeah, just a second," she said, looking at the large envelope addressed to James. Her blood pounded through her heart when she glanced up at the return address. "Oh my god! Frank, come here. Quick."

Frank shuffled his way back to Kathi, tinsel strung between his fingers. "Now what?"

"Look at this, will ya?"

Frank took the envelope, staring at her as if she'd just handed him a pot of gold. "We've got to show this to Heather, now."

"No. It's waited this long, it can wait a little longer. She needs her sleep," Kathi said, hugging and kissing her husband.

****

"Heather, wake up."

"Uh?" Rolling over, she looked at Frank sitting on the edge of her bed. "What's wrong? Have they--"

"No, nothing. But we need to talk about something," he said, looking a bit on the nervous side.

"Now?" she asked, stretching.

"How do you feel?" he asked, playing with the envelope in his hand.

"Tired. Why?" She pulled herself to a sitting position. She hadn't felt this half-alive in months. "How do you expect me to feel?"

"Well, see this letter here?" he started, handing her the envelope he'd been worrying. "You'd better look at it."

"Is it about James?" *Oh please don't let it be a death certificate or something like that. They would have called, wouldn't they?*

"Sort of, but it might concern everyone."

Heather looked into his eyes, urgency bordering them. She took the offering, turning it over and over in her hand. She couldn't bear to look at the return address. What if it was from the Montana state patrol? What if it was from a coroner's office? What if it was from...

Her veins exploded with the blood rushing through them.

She ripped open the envelope and pulled out the neatly folded piece of white stationery. Sleepiness blurring her vision, she read and then reread every single word....three times until their meaning stuck in her cloudy mind.

Unable to control herself any longer, Heather let go of the repressed fear building in her heart. She swung her legs off the bed and walked to the patio doors, pulling open the curtains. The afternoon sun spilled in for the first time in months. Her gaze never once left the piece of paper.

She felt herself being re-born, coming alive again.

****

The bathroom filled with steam. Heather stood in the shower, rotating slowing as the hot beads of water bounced off her skin. She felt her body come to life as she continuously lathered her skin with a mixture of soap and baby oil. Over and over again, she performed the routine until the past few months washed down the drain.

She'd read the letter over and over until she let it come to rest on the nightstand next to James's picture. It was then she'd given both Kathi and Frank a hug before grabbing a couple of towels on her way to the bathroom.

When she'd first seen her reflection in the full-length mirror, the image had sickened her. The circles under her eyes had grown darker from lack of sleep. Her face had thinned, becoming bony from not eating correctly. Her scowl never strayed from the reflection as she peeled off her dirty clothes making a promise to never get that low again. Not as long as she lived.

Rinsing her body one more time, Heather turned off the shower. She grabbed a towel, wrapping her now sparkling clean hair in its softness. Sliding open the door, she stepped out of the steam and into a new beginning. Her body tingled, as if it had just woken from a deep asleep. Wrapped in an oversized bath sheet, she walked out of the bathroom and into her room.

Stretched out on the brown toned comforter, Heather held James's picture in her hands, gently caressing the frame with the tips of her fingers.

"James, my love," she vowed, her voice soft and loving. "Wherever you are, know that I love you. I lost sight of myself for a while, but I'm back now…thanks to Kathi and Frank."

Her soul filled with remorse as her fingers traveled over the printed outline of James' face. "We've made it, darlin'. We've got a nomination for country video with the CMA's." She closed her eyes, sniffling. "God how I miss and love you," she whispered, pressing her lips against his printed ones, fantasizing a warm response.

She brought the photo to her breasts, feeling the thud of her beating heart against the glass. She sighed deeply and then returned the framed object of her affections to its customary resting place. Reaching for her mauve robe, she let the towel pool around her feet.

She stood at the patio doors, looking out onto the grounds of their property. She took in every tree, every blade of grass, as if seeing it for the first time. Her gaze rested on the arched branches of the trees where she'd first seen the twinkling lights of Nashville. A warm shiver ran through her. A light dusting of snow covered the very ground where James had almost made love to her. Her mind's eye saw their bodies moving in the night as they had the first time she'd come here. Committed and total love had been silently spoken between them.

"Things die, but life goes on, James," she said, looking into the grey winter sky. "Until your body's found, there's always a ray of hope. Know that I'll keep you alive in my heart and in my songs, my love, as long as I can write the words."

Chapter Thirty-Two

James's recovery from his wounds was slower than he'd thought they would be. Buck had been changing the bandages two or three times a day until he was satisfied with their healing process. Now, months after he'd been attacked by the mountain lion, James wore a shirt of animal hide and did little things around the cabin. His chest and arm muscles ached, but his strength returned more each day.

The more time the two spent together, the more James liked Buck. He knew what Buck lacked in education he made up for in many other ways. His knowledge of the mountains and living in them made James appreciate the little things in his life. He came to realize how ignorant he'd been about the world outside of the music business.

Buck recited his life chapter by chapter. He'd been coming to the mountains for over twenty years, arriving in the fall and staying until spring. He was youngest of four sons, and his parents had been part of the logging community for many years. He didn't want to be a full-time lumberjack and book learnin' was a waste of valuable time.

Buck once told James nature would teach a man all he needed to know in order to survive in the wilderness. Books couldn't teach him how to hunt and trap, or even how to last through the winter in the mountains. Only Mother Nature had the tools to do that, if the man was strong enough.

During the long, cold winter nights James and Buck sat into the night in front of the hearth. James realized his life wasn't as rough as he'd thought. He'd had parents who tried to make sure he understood everything in his life as it was, never forcing him into anything he didn't desire or have an interest in.

Then there was Buck, who'd been taught the only thing that mattered were getting trees down. He'd lived that life for too many years until a slide of trunks gone out of control killed one of his brothers. He'd been unable to cope with the loss of his brother and disappeared into the darkness one rainy night.

Stacking the wood that helped him gain his strength back, James pondered what had transpired over the past few months. How was Heather holding up? Had she declared him dead? Would they start looking for him when the mountain allowed them to? He'd looked up from his thoughts to find Buck standing in front of him with a bunch of dead animals dangling in his hand.

"Ugh." James strained, lifting the last chunk of wood on the pile leaning against the cabin. He covered it with an animal hide, protecting it from the elements.

"What you get this time?" James asked, stretching his muscles loose.

"Mostly rabbit, a raccoon or two. Small stuff, but enough," Buck flung the dead animals into the snow at James' feet. "You gonna learn how to skin these critters here."

"No way," he retorted, shock spreading through his city mind. Buck held out a hunting knife, offering it to James. Taking it, James sat cross-legged in the snow, his eyes moving from the dead animals in front of him to Buck's weathered face.

This can't be any different than fish, he thought, searching Buck's face. "I've never done this before, Buck."

"Watch 'n ya'll learn," Buck said, joining James in the snow. With the skill of a seasoned hunter, he pushed the razor-sharp blade into the belly of a rabbit. Pulling the skin back and over its head, Buck removed the insides before putting the cut and cleaned meat into a bucket of salt water.

James matched Buck's every step of the way, reenacting every movement until he completed the skinning process then moved onto another animal. Picking up a rabbit by the ears, James slid his knife awkwardly into its belly.

Buck picked up another animal, sliding a knife easily into its belly. "Ya healed real good, James," he said, peeling the fur covered skin from the meat it protected. "Ya got most of yer strength back. Can travel real soon."

"What?" James asked, leaving a disfigured rabbit lying in the crimson snow.

"Could be 'bout three weeks. Take ya down the mountain. Show ya the road to town," Buck said, continuing to cut the meat in front of him.

"You mean to tell me...?" James began, forgetting about the gutted rabbit.

"Yep," Buck said, his voice soft and low as he looked at James.

They sat searching each other's eyes. Pools of water stood in each pair, until they were blinked away. Each man had a different reason for the tears.

Chapter Thirty-Three

Heather didn't have much luggage when she checked in for her flight. There was little time to waste before the last call for her gate was announced. Her pace slowed as she reached the seating area and walked down the ramp to the plane. Taking her seat, she buckled herself in and slid on a pair of headphones. Before long, the gentle sway of the plane lulled her to sleep.

She woke from her catnap with a shiver. Looking out through the frosted window, the snow-covered ground indicated she'd be landing soon. Heather brought her seat to an upright position and watched the land below come closer and closer.

There'd be no car and driver for her this time. No one was anxiously awaiting her arrival. Just the rental car and a lonely drive along the snow-covered Wisconsin country roads.

Driving from the Madison airport, she headed north on Highway 51. The once green and lush fields were covered deep in snow. Some dried corn stalks peeked out like telescopes along the road. The setting sun shimmered off the crusty blanket making the fields look like patches of diamonds.

After about forty-five minutes, she pulled on to a long and winding driveway and stopped long enough to check the mailbox, which to her pleasure was empty. She continued up the drive, passing the fence-lined pastures toward the house. Her house.

The few horses she and James had purchased frolicked in the snow like children. The same sense of relief flooded her. Freedom.

Bringing the rental to a full stop, she got out, leaving the door slightly ajar. Closing her eyes, she took several deep, crisp breaths of the fresh, cold country air. It was so peaceful. So quiet. No one standing over her, checking her every move. Home was the perfect place for her to come to terms with everything, with herself.

Going to the stables first, she wanted to see the grounds immediately surrounding the house before getting a bite to eat. The house had remained shut up while she'd been in Nashville. Only a neighbor boy had come to feed the horses, making sure they were let out every day.

After inspection of the barn, she crawled through the fence and whistled for the horses. She continued her leisurely plodding as her gelding, Cynamon, trotted over to greet her. She nuzzled his neck, tears threatening her soul.

The sky turned dark and the air cooled. A shiver ran through her veins reminding her of the bitter cold winter day. Cynamon already headed toward the gate, her signal that they needed to be fed and bedded down for the night.

As long as she stayed, it would be up to her to do those chores. Or at least until her mind was clearer on what she should do. She needed to say goodbye to James in her own way. Not in Nashville surrounded by well-wishers, but here where they'd shared quiet and loving moments.

For now, she had horses to get in and a pantry to make sure had been fully stocked at her request.

****

For the past several weeks, Heather had awoken feeling relaxed and refreshed. She wasn't sure whether it was the clear, crisp air or being on her own. She loved being able to run around the house in pj's most of the day, especially after getting the horses bedded down for the night.

She'd taken to riding in the arena the first morning after her arrival. It gave her peace and cleared her mind of the cloud she'd been living in since October. Each morning she rode, the cloak of winter opened itself to her, taking her in. Consoling her. Helping her come to terms with life. With death.

Even Cynamon sensed the grief easing from her soul. He continually greeted her each morning with a soft nicker and a search of her coat pocket for the treat he'd grown accustomed to.

Today was different. The sun shone brightly across the pastures and the temperatures had risen to the high twenties. A perfect day to take a winter ride. Her gelding, Cynamon, had grown accustomed to her fussing with him every day. She knew he was itching as much as she was to get some real exercise and stretch his legs. Today was that day.

With the arrival of a new year, she'd come to peace with James's disappearance. It was highly unlikely that if and when he was found, it would be alive.

Entering a small meadow in the north quarter of her property, she urged her mount into a trot. She circled around the outer edge of the meadow's core, before reining the gelding in. There, she sat quietly in the saddle, and took in the surrounding tree line. It completely circled the

114

meadow.

Big puffs of snow fell through the sky like cotton balls, making her feel like a five year old again. Sliding smoothly out of her finely tooled leather seat, she stood next to the gelding, stroking his neck. A strong childish urge overtook her adult mind. She extended her arms, twirling until she became dizzy and giddy. Giggling, she lost her balance and fell into the snow. She rolled over onto her back and spread her legs back and forth in unison with her arms until she formed a perfect snow angel. She carefully removed her body from the imprint, so as not to disturb it.

Heavenly peace swept through her. The feeling found every dark passage, lighting it with a soft, warm glow. Finally, she knew what she had to do. The path was clear, leading her back to her destiny and her songs.

Remounting her horse, she sat quietly for a brief moment. Gently kicking with her heels, woman and horse rode off into the trees, the snow angel glistening in the sun and snow.

Chapter Thirty-Four

Deciding not to tell anyone back in Nashville she was returning, Heather made the necessary arrangements for the stable before taking a flight back. Exhilaration pumped through her as she made her way through the Nashville airport. She stepped through the doors and flagged down a taxi, giving him the address before turning inward to her thoughts.

She glanced at her watch. *Good. They won't be home.* She'd have plenty of time to make a surprise dinner. She closed her eyes, feeling peace and restful.

The cab pulled on to her drive, lulling her from her light dozing. "Thank you," she said, tipping the driver before lighting from the vehicle.

Pausing for a moment, Heather soaked in what really belonged to James. The house. The property. She'd never give it up or let anything happen that would cause her to lose it. This was all she physically had left of him at the moment.

Once inside, Heather flipped on the switch to the gas fireplace then headed straight for the kitchen searching through the cabinets and refrigerator for casserole items—something from almost nothing. She combined vegetables, noodles, meat, potatoes and sauce together and then placed it in the oven for thirty minutes before adding cheese to the top.

The sound of Frank's clickity old van was a perfect complement to the crackling of the wood in the fireplace. Both were cozy and filled with warmth. Heather peered out the window and then ducked behind the curtain as the van pulled nearer. Giggling, she imagined the look on Kathi's face seeing the smoke billowing from the chimney.

"She's probably panicked thinking they'd left the fireplace going all night," she giggled, watching the passenger side door fly open. Kathi jumped out of the van, running for the door.

Heather grabbed the doorknob as Kathi pushed the door open, jogging into the living room. "I swear I turned it off, Frank," Kathi called, scoping the room for damage.

Frank walked through the doorway, passing Heather without a second thought. "You got something in the oven, too?"

"That would be my dish, Frank," Heather said, standing in front of the closed door.

"What are ya doin' here?" Kathi asked, her scolding words making Heather laugh. "You should have called…and that dang smoke scared the hell out of me, Heather."

"There she goes again. Frank, you need to give this woman a child of her own so she'll stop practicing on me," Heather teased, wrapping her arms around her friend. She loved the woman like a sister, maybe even more.

"I'm glad you're here," Kathi whimpered, wiping away the tears trailing down her cheek.

"It was hard playin' twenty questions about you," Frank said, swatting Heather's backside on his way to the kitchen. "Stardom and privacy aren't good bed partners."

"Sorry. I'll explain later. Right now, let's go eat," Heather said, following Frank into the kitchen, her arm hooked into Kathi's.

The dinner conversation focused on Heather and her month in exile. She explained she'd finally found peace with James's disappearance, how she felt alive again. As she tried to communicate those feelings to her friends, she doubted they really understood. After all, Frank had been found alive; and although Kathi had felt pain she'd never felt the despair Heather had.

Heather grabbed a bottle of wine from the fridge. "Come on, we've got a perfectly good fire out there," she suggested, gathering some glasses before heading out to the living room.

"Whew, that's one thing I've missed for sure. Heather's surprise casseroles," Frank patted his slightly bulging stomach, purring like a cat.

"I'm glad you liked it. The way you kept filling your plate, no one would have guessed," she teased, patting his stomach as she settled down into James's favorite chair. James's musky scent enveloped her, warming her soul. Not too long ago, she would have burst into tears. Now it was a welcoming sensation.

"I've come to some decisions." She twirled the ruby liquid in her glass. "And to terms with James's disappearance. Being alone for the past month really helped, as did the morning rides I took each day. Being with the horses cleared my mind more than any amount of professional therapy would have," she mused, taking a sip of the wine. "It's amazing how little by little everything emerged until there was nothing but peace. The way seemed to clear; there was nothing to fear anymore." She sighed, getting up from the chair.

Standing next to the fireplace, she leaned against the mantle with one hand and looked around the room. Everything was just as it had been the day the band had left for Montana last October. Not a single article out of place.

"James is dead." The words voiced matter-of-fact. "That's all there is to it. But, that doesn't mean I have to depart from the living, too. James *will* live on through my songs. Every word I write will always have him in mind." Heather turned, looking into the faces of her stunned friends. "We have a lot of work to do. We'll need to find a new lead singer. James would want the Ramblers to keep on going, and he'll be there with each song that's sung. With each note that's struck."

"Heather, I don't know what to say," Frank muttered, his voice cracking on the edge.

"There's nothing to say, Frank. It'll be hard and we'll get through it," She gazed into the fire still warmly burning not sure what she was looking for. "We'll get the ball rolling when we get back from the AMAs and L.A."

"Welcome home, Heather," Kathi said, happiness lighting her eyes. "Welcome back."

"It's good to be home," Heather said, feeling the tears she'd fought back finally escape. She felt a new wave of doubt sweep through her. *I am doing the right thing, aren't I?*

Chapter Thirty-Five

The next week went by too quickly. The night of the American Music Association awards was less than twelve hours away. Heather had flown into Los Angeles the night before with a prayer of bringing home the one award.

She wore a simple yet elegant black dress, her blonde hair done up in a French braid with wisps of hair around her face. She kept pushing the tickling hairs away every few minutes.

Riding together in one limousine, she thanked God for the silence between them all. Her nerves popped and crackled so much, she didn't think she'd be able to say one intelligent word if she had to participate in a conversation.

Arriving at the ceremonies, they waited in line as each vehicle before them emptied out their passengers to screaming fans. Of course, she wasn't as easily recognizable, but still loved this was happening to her. At least one of her dreams was coming full circle.

Her limo pulled up, and she exited as gracefully as she could, with Frank and Kathi following behind her. The bright lights, flash bulbs, and screaming fans greeting them. She smiled and waved at the fans gathered along the red carpet until she reached the safety of the building.

Frank and Kathi caught up to her, and were about to be whisked away to their seats when someone behind them cleared his voice.

"Excuse me," an usher said, tapping Frank on the shoulder. "Mr. Whitman, I'm sorry, but I must ask you to accompany me."

"Now?"

"Yes, sir," the usher replied.

"All right." Frank shrugged his shoulders and followed the tuxedo-clad young man through the crowd.

Heather, Kathi, and the rest of the Ramblers were escorted to their seats in the fifth row. Heather looked around, noting they sat near the members of Alabama. *Holy cow, we're sitting with royalty*, she thought, drawing in a breath to calm the quake rumbling through her body.

The chattering of well wishes died down as the lights dimmed. Frank finally arrived just as the curtain was about to go up.

"What was that all about?" Heather heard Kathi ask, echoing her thoughts.

Not taking his eyes off the stage, he turned and whispered back, "Nothin' important. You know Utah. Some sort of a mix-up. Sh-sh."

The opening music began and the master of ceremonies welcomed everyone to the show. Heather sat calmly in her seat, silently crying out for James. She soon became lost in her thoughts of life with and without him.

Am I doing the right thing?

How many times was she going to ask herself the same question over and over again?

She automatically clapped as award after award was handed out. She glanced over, feeling Frank's eyes on her. She smiled, hoping he'd take it as a sign she was doing okay.

"Emerald Braun and Utah Sheridan!" the voice over the PA announced.

Applause thundered as Emerald and Utah walked hand in hand up to the podium, smiling from ear to ear. They were country's newest couple, love radiating off them.

"Thank you," they said in unison, perfectly in tuned with each other.

"Blake, we're here to award the Favorite Video of the Year to one of five great performers," Amanda announced, tapping the envelope on the podium.

"And the field has been on fire this year, Em," Utah said, winking at his partner.

"Right, so let's get on with it," Emerald replied.

"Okay, the nominees for Favorite Country Video are…"

The first four nominees were announced, followed by clips of their videos.

"And our fifth and final nomination is *Whispering Wind* by James Sheridan and the Night Ramblers."

Frank nudged her slightly, snapping her out of the daze she'd been in. She watched through tears as James came to life on the screen. How well she remembered the filming of that video. They'd had to wait for weeks before the sky and clouds were just right.

"And the winner is…" Emerald began, nervously ripping open the envelope then grabbing Utah's arm. "*Whispering Wind* by James Sheridan and the Night Ramblers!"

Frank let out a yelp and Kathi hugged a stunned Heather.

"Here to accept the award for James Sheridan is Heather Jones-

Sheridan."

Her name came crisply over the PA system as she stood on shaking legs. Moving slowly, yet hurriedly through the people, she gracefully climbed the few steps to the stage. Falling into the embraces of Utah, she held the award in her hand as *Whispering Wind* played softly in the background. Tears flowed freely and she cleared her throat.

"Thank you. Thank you all very much. Who better than your brother-in-law to announce your name! Um, as you all know James can't physically be with us tonight. He disappeared after an accident and..." Heather fought to get a hold of her emotions shifting her weight from one leg to another. "I know that wherever he is, he'd want to thank Frank Whitman for his musical talents as well as the Night Ramblers, who never gave up hope. He'd also want you all to know..."

The music for *Snowy Firelight* began and a queer hush fell over the crowd. Heather stared in bewilderment at the crowd. Thunderous applause drowned out James's first number one song.

"It's okay, Heather," Utah whispered into her ear, his hand lightly on her elbow. "There's someone here to see you."

Turning, Heather watched a strange-looking man amble toward her. His hair was long and shaggy while the growth on his face showed several months of being unkempt. His dress was that of a long-ago fur trader.

She placed a hand on the podium as the distance between them lessened. To the left of the stage, in the shadows behind the stranger stood Frank, Kathi, and the band. Heather stood rooted in her place, unable to move or think.

The crowd sat as quiet as church mice as the stranger stopped halfway across the stage. Heather's blurred eyes finally focused in on the ones that longingly and lovingly looked at her with intimate familiarity. Her knees grew week. Her heart skipped a beat and then briefly stopped before coming to pounding life.

"James?" Heather asked, her voice soft and confused. She cautiously stepped closer to the man, standing several feet away from her. "James!" she yelled, running full steam into the arms of the man who was her whole world.

Their eyes locked on each other. "I told a friend of mine I had to be in Nashville by morning, no matter what the weather." James's weather-beaten lips took her soft ones, and their salty tears mingled. Their kiss was deep and lasted forever.

When they left the stage locked in each other's arms, they knew their love for love songs had brought them together, but faith and faith alone would keep them together...always.

~ The End ~

ABOUT THE AUTHOR

 Maxine Douglas first began writing in the early 1970s while in high school. She took every creative writing course that was offered (grammar was not her best course) at the time and focused her energy for many, many years after that time on poetry. When a dear friend's sister revealed she was going to become a published romance author, that was all Maxine needed to get the ball rolling. She finished her first manuscript in a month's time.

Maxine currently resides in Oklahoma with her husband, and is a member of Romance Writers of America, Oklahoma Romance Writers of America, and the Oklahoma Writer's Federation, Inc.

One of the many things Maxine has learned over the years of her life is that you can never stop dreaming and reaching for the stars, because sooner or later, you'll touch one, and it'll bring you more happiness than you can ever imagine. She feels lucky and blessed, over the past several years, to have been able to reach out and touch the stars—and she's still reaching.

Maxine loves hearing from her readers. All you have to do is catch her at Facebook, Twitter@waMaxineDouglas, or her blog. Come on over and say "Hello."

Hugs! Maxine Douglas

BOOK EXCERPTS/PRAISE

Nashville Rising Star

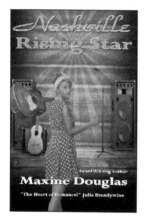

Lights and music became one, and excitement built inside Emerald, the sensation to sway seductively to the music something new to her otherwise quiet existence before entering the competition. As usual, Utah made her listen to and feel every word he sang. His voice drew her deeper into the strange sensation building inside her, sensual to the point of making her throb in a place she ached to have him warm up.

When the song ended, Utah waved and bowed to the audience. Then he and jogged off stage in her direction. With a sultry smile on his mouth, he tipped his hat at her as he drifted past as if he knew and laughed at the riot he'd caused in her body. A flush of goose bumps crept through her as he brushed by her. The shivers felt more like a warning than anything else. He was way too complicated, and Emerald knew she needed to leave him alone.

> 5 Stars! Maxine Douglas has a way of writing heartwarming romance that will keep you turning the pages until the sweet ending.
> *by Julia Brandywine, Author*

> 5 Stars! Like a special piece of chocolate candy, this delightful sweet romance short story will please your reading palate.
> *by Lorna Collins, Award Winning Author*

Road Angel

As the snow swirls in the glow of the headlights, I figure several inches have fallen on top of what may have been tire marks in the road. I don't even want to think when it was plowed last. At this rate, I probably won't see one until tomorrow.

The wind howls continuously around the cab of the tractor and bangs against the doors. With each new gust, the trailer slides slightly, giving in to the force. The blowing wind sings a wolf melody, the howling tune mournful—a beautiful yet deadly blizzard accompanied by the music of the wind—Mother Nature's way of easing the cruelty she sometimes gives so freely.

Snow like this can play tricks on a man's vision. Even knowing this, when I see a figure in the middle of the road, reaction takes over reasoning. White and flowing, it moves toward me, and then silver-blue eyes bore into my soul, making me yearn for sweet oblivion. In that swift moment, I swerve, my mind screaming out the name of the woman who left my world three years before.

Sandi!

Guardian Angel Third Class Cynamon Bedford watches in horror from her snow-packed seat perched near the gates of Heaven the crash the phantom causes. The cherry-red semi-truck's tires screech to grab solid ground. Metal crashes and crunches as the truck slides on its side across the road. The screeching tears at her heart; the driver, Lee Thomas, has a slim chance of making it.

The crumpled mass of cherry red, a deadly contrast to the snow, lays in an L shape down the slope between the road and a line of trees. The cab faces the way it has just come from, cheery Christmas music fading in and out, a maudlin contrast. The windshield shattered, glass is scattered across the snow drifts. Snow quickly blankets the wreck.

There is nothing she can do. Helpless, she sits and watches as another life slowly disappears from Earth. "If only they understood how precious their time is, maybe the mortals wouldn't be so careless with the gift." One silvery tear makes a slow trek down her cheek as she feels the dying man's pain.

Blood Ties

"Okay, so maybe I'm crazy, but I know very well the scent of lavender when I smell it. I grew up with it all over this house."

"Did you ever think that maybe your clothes picked up the scent somewhere?"

Emma felt him closing in behind her. His maleness played with her senses. She was losing her ability to be sensible and keep this a business arrangement. Her mission was to find out about Aunt Manda, not seduce the owner of the house.

Faster, she told herself, *I've got to move faster. Must reach the back stairs before he catches up with* me.

Her heart picked up speed and she shivered as her skin grew clammy with panic making its way through her. The urge to be in his arms, to feel the touch of his lips on her skin intensified the animal urges she didn't know dwelled in her spirit.

Royal grabbed Emma by the arm, swinging her around and into his chest.

"Only if I had doused myself in it," he said.

The feel of his arms around her proved to be the kindling to refuel the fire already ignited in her soul. Royal's eyes held a burning rage of desire within their depths. His lips parted slightly, then spoke to her of the promises meant for her only as he kissed her. She melted like the Wicked Witch of the West from the pleasure his mouth gave. If he thought her to be a spell maker, than he certainly had to be Merlin, for he was the one casting spells.

Emma's heart beat in unison with his. Their breathing became one as the embrace grew stronger, closer with each spark generated from their lips. His mouth caressed hers in a skillful manner. She hungered to feel his kisses on more than just her delightfully pulsing lips.

Now this isn't so bad, is it Emma? The whispered words ran in her mind. *He must have read your thoughts, seen your desires reflecting in your eyes, Emma. I didn't think Royal had it in him anymore.*

Emma took a step backwards and lost her balance. The hall moved in slow motion before her bottom hit the floor with a muffled thump. She didn't dare look up at Royal. She didn't know if it was the fall or the kiss that had caused the warm feeling that burned her cheeks. She took hold of the hand Royal extended to her with reluctance.

The Queen

He's come for you at last, Hanna. Bill, my Bill. Here aboard the ship? Reluctantly, Hanna Amery keeps her distance from him, fading into the background, yet wanting so badly to touch the man she had given her heart to. Admittedly, he looked a bit different now, his ebony skin now a light milk chocolate, his once thin body more muscular but she could feel Bill's spirit inside him. She aches to reach out and let him know she was there waiting for him like she'd promised. From the moment he'd walked out onto the deck heading toward the Isolation Ward she'd felt his presence. His spirit felt as strong today as it was seventy years ago when they first met, and it called to her bringing her back to the present.

The steel railing was cold and damp in my warm hand as I strode down the deck, trying to ignore the tingling at my back. Like some spirit was watching me. *Get used to it, it's your job.* Still, it felt deep, personal. A wisp of a chill passed through me at the thought and the soft feminine words, "yes it is," echoed forlornly through my mind. What the hell…now I was hearing ghosts. I rushed along in a hurry to get below deck.

Peering into the dim, yellowish light cast over the iron steps, I looked back straining to see the presence that may have touched my soul for a brief moment. The light scent of lavender perfume and the faint sounds of swing music drifted over to me. Inhaling deeply I closed my eyes feeling transported back to the war years, hearing the moans of the sick, the tender voices of the nurses, the motion of the ocean. Shivering, I opened my eyes deliberately pulling away from someone else's memories. I couldn't let myself fall into the past or I might not come back. *Where the hell had that thought come from? You're the ghost disprover remember? Get it together man,* I told myself then turned and descended into what may have been a living hell for some soldiers.

"Wonderful story, passionate and compelling…."
by Alicia Dean, Award Winning Author

Rings of Paradise

"Khristen." Someone repeated her name, and as she stirred, raised his voice, calling to her again.

"Huh?" Sleepy eyed and well-burnt, Khristen was not sure what had drawn her out of a groggy sleep.

"What's your pleasure? Mai Tai, Piña Colada, or Aloe Vera?" Shadoe adjusted the two sweating glasses and one bottle on the tray he balanced with care.

Khristen shielded her eyes, suspiciously looking up at him. The touch of friendly sarcasm that had edged his over-exaggerated deep voice set off her warning light.

"Owweeee!" Pain and agony edged her voice, caused from the effects of too many hours in the sun and too little sunscreen.

"I've got just what you need."

"Like what?" Khristen grimaced, seeing the bottle of lotion and look of concern in his eyes.

Or is it lust?

"RINGS OF PARADISE is an awesome read and I will tell my friends all about it!!!"
by Racegirl

"RINGS OF PARADISE is a superbly told, sexy romance. I'll be looking for more books by Maxine Douglas soon."
by Cheryl C. Malandrinos

"...the story was really good that I cannot give it a lower rating than a 5."
by SmallMallReads

"RINGS OF PARADISE is a superbly told, sexy romance. I'll be looking for more books by Maxine Douglas soon."
by The Book Connection

Knight to Remember

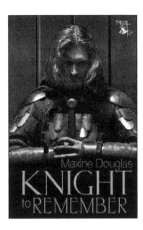

Unexpected jealousy had flooded Courtney when she'd overheard the hushed whispers of the women talking about Reynold as they looked through her dresses, fantasizing about what they could do to him. Their description of Reynold's expertise with a lance and his handling of Abraxas made her blood boil. She wanted to rip the garments out of their grasping fingers and tell them to never come back to her shop again as long as she lived. She couldn't. She had no right, and even if she did, it was nothing more than a performance for the outside world. These women meant as much to him as she did...which was nothing.

Shaking the earlier scene from her mind, Courtney crossed her arms over her midsection. Leaning back, she wondered what in the world she was doing. She didn't have to be here today. She didn't have to leave her shop in the very capable hands of young summer help. But she had, and there was no turning back, no trying to sneak away without someone she knew recognizing and stopping her. No, she'd made the decision to watch the last joust, and she'd just have to stay with it. Her palms damp and her body in a cold sweat, Courtney watched and listened as the knights' squires on the other side of the arena pumped up the crowd with their poetic verse. Each squire was responsible for a section of the bleachers, instructing the people there on whom to cheer for and how to cheer.

Talk about men in tights...

There was plenty implied to inflame a woman's imagination under those crotch-length tunics. She was sure each of them enjoyed showing his package without really exposing himself.

The fanfare signaled the ceremony as Queen Victoria and her ladies in waiting entered the viewing area set aside for the royalty of Bristol's Heartsease. Queen Victoria acknowledged the rest of her court, waved to her royal subjects seated across the dirt arena, and then took her seat under the wooden pavilion.

Courtney watched the re-enactors take their royal places. Queen Victoria motioned for the audience to be silent. It would only be a matter of moments now before the scripted competition started. She'd finally find out what the female shoppers in her shop had gotten so hot and bothered about.

Although she could just about imagine. Even without the armor,

Reynold had the body to stir even the deepest hidden desires. He'd certainly succeeded in stirring her blood without asking. If he had asked, would she have given herself over to him so easily? Probably not. She wanted her knight to be hers and hers alone. She just wasn't into sharing.

"…I LOVED this book. From the opening challenge and evil edict issued by the impudent and cruel queen, to the modern world…"
by Lady Bug Lin

"…Well-written and fast-paced, Reynold and Courtney's adventures kept me turning the pages."
by Edith

Writing as Debi Wilder

Human Touch

Gabby's Second Chance

Blue Moon Magic (print only)

By the Blue Moon (ebook coming soon)

eBooks can be found at

MuseItUpPublishing or MuseItHotPublishing

Amazon or Barnes and Noble.

42614159R00077

Made in the USA
Middletown, DE
16 April 2017